BACKSTAGE
CREW

WRITINGS BY

MARY-ANA-CHELSEA-JOEL
NICHOLS-GREG-JO-MANSHIP-CELLO
LUKA-JIM&LESLIE-ALBERT-KIM-KASIA
AND SUZKA

Copyright © 2017 Suzka

All rights reserved.

ISBN-13: 978-1975888015
ISBN-10: 1975888014

DEDICATED TO
PAUL VIEREGGE AND MIKE WILMOT

BACKSTAGE

CONTENTS

1. BACKSTAGE ROYALITY…. page 3
2. INTRODUCTION by Suzka…. page 17
3. GREG FLOOR…. page 25
4. J O – JANET OWENS…. page 27
5. MIKE MANSHIP…. page 33
6. CELLO VITASOVIC…. page 41
7. LUKA VITASOVIC…. page 67
8. GARDEN STAGE…. page 73
9. JIM AND LESLIE…. page 77
10. ALBERT CHRISTY…. page 79
11. KIM CANDLER…. page 85
12. KASIS ZAJAC…. page 87
13. SUZKA…. page 89
14. JOHN NICHOLS…. page 97
15. And More Pictures….

ACKNOWLEDGMENTS

Cover and Design by Suzka

Selected Photos by John Nichols

Stories Written by
Monterey Jazz Festival
Crew Members

ANNA VIEREGGE DAVEY, MARY VIEREGGE, CHELSEA AND GREG DAVEY

1
SECOND GENERATION ROYALITY

MARY VIEREGGE

What is the Monterrey Jazz Festival to me? It's the second Saturday of September when the cars start rolling across that wooden bridge to the Log cabin in Big Sur, the hugs of the family that migrates to the same destination this time of year, for as long as I can remember. It's a reflection of a lifelong friendship between Paul Vieregge and Mike Wilmot. It's the sleepy tired, half hung over bodies that are the first to arrive in Monterey to assemble the pieces and sweep the stage. It is Monday night football in Wilmot's or Paul's room at the Travel Lodge. It's the smell of Leon's barbeque wafting across the fairgrounds into the arena as we try to slap on those final brushes of color to the become the backdrop to new and old jazz traditions. It's the Wednesday which Doc goes down to the wharf and scores some fresh tuna to make sushi on the main stage. It's the slide shows of last year's festival. It is the jokes and laughter Thursday after the stage crew barbeque when we roll on over to the empty arena and watch the light crew add their touches to the set.

For me the Jazz Festival has never been about the music it has been about Paul Vieregge (my father) and my relationship with him and his relationship with the world of jazz. It was while my father was dying I learned the importance of the festival and how it was the background to his personal life. It was the one thing he had as a constant wherever his journey of life would take him. No matter where he was come September he had a foundation, which restored him and brought music to others. The tunes from his record collection echoed from the rafters of the cabin in Big Sur. These records, my dad never purchased, each and every one was given to him by the artist themselves.

The week leading to the music is where the Jazz festival lives in me. It wasn't until I got older and went out into the world that I learned MJF was global and not just a ditty we played in our back yard.

One Thursday night in the arena my Dad told me a story of three guys who had a vision and the only place they could find to manifest this dream was a little horse arena south of San Francisco in a town called Monterey. So Paul, Jimmy and Ralph went to the bank of America and got a loan for $1,000.00, from that loan the first Monterey Jazz festival was born.

In the beginning we lived in Sausalito and my Father would head down the week before. Then We, Penny and us three kids, would take the train to Monterey on Thursday for Leon's barbeque. At that time my Childs memory only holds the visual of a model train at the del Monte express, a burger joint at the train station. Followed by the pool at the travel lodge and Leon's big smoky hugs.

As the jazz festival and us kids grew so did the traditions that wrap around it. These traditions link together this extended family that migrated from every corner of the map to become a force, which forged a collaboration known as the Monterey jazz festival.

In the beginning I don't think everyone had actually planned to keep coming back the following year. I think it was the for sure way that Paul would just look at each person on the way out and say " see you next year" like there was no doubt. It was like this door was always open to the looking glass into the next Jazz festival.

There was a women, her name was Morgan she wore all black, drove a white Porsche, she was clad in cameras and spoke threw the sound of her shutter. Every year on Wednesday we would gather on the stage to watch her slide show. We see ourselves flashed up on a make shift screen and comment on how much we changed and grew over the last year since our last gathering on this stage. From this the questioned arose...what and where do we do our lives the other 11 months of the year? So the slide show evolved to a 'who are you' when you are not here slide show, and for the next year a different person was chosen to put together a slide show.

Laurel Lyon's was always one of my favorite persons. She had an air of rebellious elegance. She smoked these thin little cigarettes and had a laugh that was contagious. As a young girl I wanted to be like her. She and Jimmy would jet set in from Japan. Laurel after flying all night would still look fresh and glamorous. She would make her way to the Hunt Club order her Smirnoff on the rocks and her social circle would start to gather around her table. I remember the first time I was invited to stop at her table, I felt I had made it through the rite of passage; I was no longer a child.

After Jimmy had passed there was this night Laurel came down to the house in Bug Sur, for some reason my parents weren't home. Being the women she was, so young at heart she spent the evening with us teenagers. At some point in the evening we ended up sitting on the Big Sur cliffs above the ocean. It was one of those amazing Big Sur nights where the Santa Ana winds were blowing the moon was full. There she told of stories of her and Jimmy's life finally cried and let him go. It was an honor for the children to be there for her at this time. I will always cherish my memories of her, in some sort of way Ms. Laurel helped develop the women I am today. She set an example on how to be yourself and to strive to keep your head up no matter what the odds life throws at you are.

BACKSTAGE

Growing up backstage there becomes a certain point where you are no longer just a child running around the arena and you become a useful part of the team. It normally starts with picking up a paint brush, or a broom. From there it progresses to actually being given a start time to show up at work, not just rolling in whenever you feel like it. This is how most of the next generations started. Our functions then morphed into trying out multiple positions throughout the years. Performing task such as, curtain pager, Jotting down start and stop times of the sets, which for some reason was incredibly important. Who knows if these notes were ever saved, more or less archived? I think all of us were drivers for Dave at some point. Oh the stories I could tell of my two seasons as a young driver. Like the time I got a ticket with Diana Reeves in the car. Oh, I once dropped JJ. Johnsen off at the hotel and forgot to get his horn out of the trunk. Then there was Clark Terry the man of absolute kindness and elegance. Clark had the magic of making you feel like you were special as if he had been your friend your entire life. There were also some horrible faux pas I made working back stage, like closing the curtain on Grover Washington Jr. or not opening the door to the stage for Dizzy Gillespie to start his set.

A couple of us actually ended up choosing theater arts as a profession. Both Joel and I attended the pacific Conservatory of the Arts. In 1989 armed with the completion of my PCPA education I came to the Jazz Festival as a lighting designer. At this time, moving lights were a new thing in the world of concerts. So I was going to change the stage of the Monterey Jazz festival and actually have a design, not just a wash. For my first Thursday ever I was working on the stage focusing the lights with the union crew, while my family partied it up at heckled from the arena. Mike Wilmot was my biggest advocate and grave me free range. There was one problem with my rock and roll lighting...I had failed to take the camera into consideration. This issue was soon remedied with some newly position front of house lights. Then it was Showtime, there I was in the lighting booth above stage right moving color all over that stage. As exciting as this was for me my father, being an old school television man, was not nearly as pleased with all this other jazz going on around the stage. For Paul Vieregge it was about the musicians. The music was so strong and powerful the message was in the notes. My Lights only distracted from the purity of the performance. I did move on and continue my professional life as a lighting designer. I was blessed to have my career take me around the globe. Because of the comfort I learned backstage at the Monterey Jazz Festival I was able to create an ambiance for many performances, I always said, "I paint music and create visual dimensions."

Then would come Sunday night when the final curtain came down and McCune started their load out. We would all convene in the back alley between the main stage and the office to reminisce over the weekend, smoke cigars, taste some whiskey and say our good-byes. While in the background Penny plays Bach on one of the festivals finely tuned pianos.

If you walk down this alley today you will see a street sign, this ally has been named the Paul Vieregge Way.

The backstage of the Monterrey Jazz festival exist in the acts of love. Such as Mike Manship taking my then 19 year old brother with him back to Salt Lake. Greg Floor and Janet Owens opening their home to us wayward kids when we were searching for a new place to call home. My parents driving out to Salt Lake to be part of Greg an J.O's wedding. Mike Wilmot, Penny, Paul and myself driving a beat up 510 Datsun to telluride for the blue grass festival. Chelsea and Giles growing up backstage, Joel following in our father's footsteps, Cello getting married on the deck of the cabin in Big Sur, the Jazz fest is a continuance that spans generations.

So I think what makes the MJF uniquely different is that there isn't truly a "Backstage" we can jot down our thoughts about. Backstage to the Monterey jazz festival is not a physical place, it lives in our hearts. The crew of the Monterey jazz festival may gather at the fairgrounds year after year to create an atmosphere, which truly the essence of what a family is.

It is a Legacy, that which is given freely for no recompense.

It is the sound track to my Fathers life.

— Mary Vieregge

ANA VIEREGGE DAVEY

My first memories are of my father Paul Vieregge and his friends, all they talked about was Jazz. His friends were; Jimmy Witherspoon, John Lewis, Jimmy Lyons, Charlie Parker, Bill Grahman, Charles Mingus. They would throw a party ever year.

One of his friends was Leon. He would cook the Family BBQ on the Thursday night before the show. Every year I got to shop with Leon, its the late sixties, we would walk hand in hand, very large black man with a very small blonde girl, he would walk slow so I could keep up. On our walk we passed the Coca cola factory, it took up half the block the front was all windows, so you could watch all the bottles go by on a belt, up to the street behind it. Then we would walk by the Perry Brothers all you can eat buffet. The sign was very large, you could see it for blocks, the boys with their blonde hair, pink cheeks and plaid shirts, very Norman Rockwell. This is one of my first memories of the third weekend in September. I would do many more Thursday BBQs with Leon and have the best family and traditions to grow up with.

A lot is done to set up the Jazz Festival and the same talented people that worked together doing lights and sound for my father's crew are the ones that would show up at my parents house the week before to work setting up the stages and seats in the arena. It was a lot of work to transform the horseshow arena into a Jazz venue.

If you showed up at the canyon BBQ, you could work for my father. So that Saturday night we never knew who was going to show up, it was all word of mouth, no cell phones or wi-fi, they would just come. The stories of who and how they got there, is a book into itself.

Then one year there it was THE CREW and the promise to come back next year was said to my father by this crew was made for many more years, marriages, children, losses and love. My Family just got bigger

We all grew up together.

BACKSTAGE

Every week before the show each year, now that there were always same crew, and of course who ever else showed up in the canyon, we would get so excited to catch up on each others lives. We made pizza night and picked a person each year to show us about their lives when not at the festival. I think learning these stories made me want to travel learn and explore, incredible people. We would watch the Monterey Pop Festival movie and burn matches at the Jimi part and all would say the part in the movie "has anyone seen Paul? Where is Paul?" yes they were looking for my Dad he was there too.

On Thursday night the BBQ got bigger, and the best part was seeing the slide show that the photographer Morgan took of ALL of us working, laughing getting caught candidly, we laughed our way through dinner. All of us would walk together to the arena this is the light check night, and the first night we can see the Art we painted lit up.

It was always the last time we could sit together drink Dickle and get ready to throw the party, some times we wouldn't see each other till Sunday, Everyone is so busy running stages and watching magic.

My father's best friend is Mike Wilmot, he worked with Dad at KGO TV as a director like my father, and his son Joel became our brother. Mike learned the Main stage and worked it with my Dad, My childrens' father Greg Davey learned from them and runs the Dizzy stage, Joel learned from all of them. When my father handed Mike the Main stage his son Joel was his assistant. Joel now is teaching my daughter Chelsea Davey, who is third generation to run the main stage. My son Giles works and learns from his Dad and will for years to come. My mother Penny enjoys everything and is unstoppable trying to be at ever stage and watch all the acts. She plays the piano every Sunday night; when the people are gone, when the arena is empty, when the stage is quite. She is very talented, the music and the setting beautiful. I believe she has started a tradition herself for the Jazz musicians. They come to listen to her.

There is a gathering of thanks and good-bye's in the oak room and the promise to come back next year.

This year we are adding the fourth generation, the family and legacy grows and continues.

We all are following in very big footprints and even bigger hearts.

All of these traditions are the notes of my life song.
IT IS JAZZ

– Ana Vieregge Davey

CHELSEA DAVEY

I was born in June of 1986 so I was three months old at my first Festival and at 30 years of age I have yet to miss one. I have always known that I was privileged to be born into an extended family and heir to a family legacy that as more Festivals go by my good fortune is only amplified. The MJF Stage Family rarely see one another during the year, until everyone makes their pilgrimage back to our dusty, old fairgrounds and Travelodge Hotel the third week of September. We kick off the week and welcome the weary travelers the Saturday prior to the show at our homestead in Big Sur for the MJF Stage Crew Reunion BBQ. My memories of this party vary, when I was younger they were a raucous event that went late into the night. My Poppas Paul Vieregge and the guys would drink red wine and talk about the various shows they worked. My younger brother Giles and I would always peter out long before the adults were done "catching up" and we would often crash in the bedroom below the house to the sounds of laughter, feet stomping on the deck above and of course bebop music on the outdoor speakers. Now that so many years have gone by and some of our elders have passed, the BBQ peters out long before my brother and I do.

I suppose my first memory of the Festival is painting the Main Stage backdrop in the late 80s, which appropriate to 80s design was done with sponges dipped in different colors slapped all over the wall, perfect for a toddler. As a professional artist today, I can say without hesitation that the hand painted mural that dresses the wall of the Lyon's Stage is responsible for my love of painting. In high school I began to take painting and design very seriously, and would skip school so that I could paint the full day. It was always a treat to come into town from Big Sur during the school week and play Jazz hooky. During the day the stage is busy with activity, speaker tests, scissor lifts and loud generators, and there is a dance between the painting crew and the sound and lighting crews. For the past handful of years Susan and I will return to the grounds after everyone has left for the day, and night has fallen to light project and trace the letters "Monterey Jazz Festival" on the nearly completed wall. There is a certain quiet magic that buzzes through the night air when there are only two people on this famous stage. The airplanes pass closely overhead and their lights flash across the thousands of empty metal chairs in the arena while chilly fog spills over the balcony walls. I feel as though I have this special secret and pride knowing I helped paint the stage, and during the weekend when the audience fills the arena, sunshine beats down on all of the Festival hats, the multitude of world renowned artists and their music fill the air I sit back and enjoy that artful secret behind them. Even though the Festival happens once a year, the Jazz obsession in the house was a year round topic of conversation. My Poppas punctuated the day with new records he was discovering and our family dinners were often listening sessions to stories of the early days of the Festival. When I was 22 I moved into a house in Monterey, and when I told him the location he asked me if there was still a little red house across the street. I said that there was, and in classic fashion he had a heavy hitter name drop:

" We threw Louis Armstrong a birthday party in that little red house and served red beans and rice".

My father Greg was given the position of stage manager of Dizzy's Den for the stage's inaugural year and has been so each year since. My brother and I have grown up at "The Den". The Salinas Room is a long barn like building with cement floors and high ceilings on the other end of the fairgrounds from the Lyon's Stage. We would all pitch in, and roll yards and yards of heavy maroon carpet out, taping the edges down. Dad, my brother Giles, Uncle Ed, Kim, Jeremy, Kasha and me… the Dizzy's crew would spend an afternoon setting up 800+ chairs and wiping the fairgrounds dust from them. This work translates to some serious quality time together as a family and even though it would appear grueling, it is a special time filled with familiar laughter. We carried the same level of reverence for each artist that made their way over to us from other stages, and are often booked with a more colorful selection of music straying away from classic jazz and branching out to funk, soul, Latin and more. We have been known to clear out the front rows of chairs and allow for dancing, which in some more serious jazz environments doesn't happen often. Artists often join us at the Den following their sets on the main stage, they and their instruments are given that classic golf cart ride across the festival grounds and get to play a more intimate stage. The folks in the front row at Dizzy's Den are so close to the musicians they can almost reach out and touch them. I feel that same way someone sitting in the front row at The Den does… my life has been so close to the MJF, the people, the sounds, the traditions, the festival food, and the family…If I close my eyes I can almost reach out and touch it.

Sincerely,
Chelsea Belle Davey

JOEL WILMOT

I am Joel Wilmot, currently the Production Stage Manager and trying to fill some BIG multigenerational shoes.

Its fun to say my first festival was in 1970, 11 months old. It doesn't mean much in the practical sense but it speaks to the core of those of us in the group we call stage crew. It hints at the idea that this is a family affair. Three generations. That's how long some of the family lines go back. And that's how long we have been doing this. Together.

A quick over view of my personal time line goes like this. For various reasons I began coming in earnest to the festival in 1981. I was 12. Since then I have only missed one show in 1983 (my memory is hazy but that should be pretty accurate). Around 1985, I think I started to pitch in with the folks at the Garden Stage. I did a couple years there. Then @ 18 I helped out David Murray and was a driver. One year was plenty.

The next few years varied mainly saw me working during the week and floating. Progressively getting pushed more towards the main stage. Surprisingly the strongest pushing came from Paul. Somewhere around 1995 (I really am terrible with dates) I began my stay on the main stage. By this time the show has grown to 4 full venues.

So this is where a story should come in... Chatting with the super nice guy willing to talk to a 12year old kid sitting next to the spiral stairs. Gently interrupting suddenly with a quick excuse me! Picking up a horn from the table and walking on stage. He played a couple tunes with Bill Berry and the kids. Only to come straight back when he was done and pick up where we left off. To this day Clark Terry was one of the nicest people I ever met. ...Helping Dizzy find his room at the Hyatt, he was lost but to be fair, the bungalows are confusing... When George Benson's crew were standing toe to toe with my dad and several of us from the crew behind him. They were discussing why the curtain closed on George, it was very heated on one side. My dad being who he was just listened calmly, but repeatedly told him they had gone way over. He could be the most disarming person. You don't even realize its happening till it's over. A couple of us remarked afterwards at how close it came to blows. But my dad just smiled it off and thanked us for the support. In the 35 years I have been living the festival it has given me stories. It has given me an education. It has challenged me. It has made me suffer. And it's given me a home. The most important aspect of the festival to me is family.

So the real story is the crew. It's their stories that make us who we are. We are a group of people who come together once a year to put on a show. Most of whom this is the only time they are professionals in this business. We were collected together by a few people because they saw in us not only an interest in the music let alone love, but more importantly there was something in each that they trusted. There has been an ethos instilled that for some has been a subtle and others of us not so much. It's that the experience the artist will have here, if they are open to it, will be unique. We don't get there every time but we try. Everyone in their own way is dedicated to making sure the artists feel welcome and supported so they can do their jobs and hopefully more. These people are family. And while you are with us so are you.

In this collection of stories I hope you will get a sense of who we are and why we all keep coming back. For me it's my father. My daughters may be my contribution to the list of 3rd generationers to experience this thing we do if they want. And I hope I can impart half the experience that my father shared with me. We have a fourth generation entering the world right around the time these stories are being collected. And it makes me smile at the possibilities.

My dad shared lots of wisdom and even more b.s. But a favorite line he used was sure to make you smile, but for those in the know it was a bit more. Read it as it was told. With honesty and love.

"It may be a dump, but it is OUR dump."

– Joel Wilmot

PHOTOS BY J. NICHOLS

BACKSTAGE

PHOTO BY SUZKA

2

INTRO

    I remember exactly when it all started. I was sitting in Portofino's, a coffee house for the creatives on the Peninsula, getting my morning octane and paging through the local newspaper at the same time. It was then and there, right in front of me, an article regarding the announcement of the new general manager for the Monterey Jazz Festival. Jimmy Lyons, the previous manager, died that year. Next to the article was a small picture of Tim Jackson - a nice picture of a man with a likable face. He could have been my cousin. He looked very approachable. *'That's what I need to do, the stages. I've been to the Jazz festival, once. I saw that stage.'* For sure, this was a sign. The more time that went by, the more stage painting I did in my head. It was on that day... the back wall on the main stage at the Monterey Jazz Festival... became mine. I just needed to talk to that Tim guy and let him know.

The next day I went to the fair grounds, walked around, grounding my own creative ideas. Behind the arena stage was an office, I assumed for the Monterey Jazz Festival even though there was no sign. Without much calculated thinking on my part, I walked directly to the outside door. After a few hard knocks a gentleman opened the door. I introduced myself and told the man that I was a good friend of Tim Jackson and wondered if he was in. *"Just wanted to touch base"*. I am sure this entire conversation lasted about a minute or less but I felt like my words were creating traction and moving into an incredible recollection of bullshit. My alleged connection to Tim was unstoppable. When I felt this was going to a bad place, a voice inside my head told me to shut up already. I did stop. Time was traveling on a silent rocky road. The kind man answered after my last words hit the ground and went running into the cracks of the sidewalk like soldiers running into a foxhole after an attack.

"I am Tim Jackson."

And it was on September 13, 1993 when I first stepped onto the main stage at the Monterey Fair Grounds becoming an official member of the stage crew for the Monterey Jazz Festival. I was a bit scared to meet this tight-knit group. I hadn't a clue what to expect. I was the outsider, the uninvited, un-inherited crewmember moving into this sacred fraternity.

– Suzka (Susan) Collins

BACKSTAGE

BACKSTAGE

PHOTO BY J. NICHOLS: l. JIMMY LYONS, r. PAUL VIEREGGE

Jimmy Lyons, Ralph Gleason and Dave Brubeck started the Monterey Jazz Festival in 1958. Gleason was the stage manager. Paul Vieregge did the stage lighting. Almost immediately, Paul became the stage manager. Paul worked at KGO. That is where he met Jimmy and Mike Wilmot. The rest is history...

BACKSTAGE

PHOTO BY J. NICHOLS: l. MILT FRANKEL, r. PAUL VIEREGGE

PHOTO BY J. NICHOLS: MIKE WILMOT

PHOTO BY J. NICHOLS

PHOTOS BY J. NICHOLS: JOSH VIEREGGE

BACKSTAGE

BACKSTAGE

PHOTO BY J. NICHOLS: GREG FLOOR

3
GREG FLOOR 1973

1st Day on the Job: Summer 1973... Monterey County Fairgrounds Arena. "Well, kid, I'll bring you on at a hundred and a half for the week," commented Paul Vieregge after a fifteen-minute interview (set up by Mercedes Bradley) in the dusty, flea jumping, manure spattered arena. I hit the big time and had just been hired to work the 15th Annual Monterey Jazz Festival.

So this is where the people hang out for the famous MJF I thought to myself. It kind of reminded me of an open-air hippie rock festival I went to a few years earlier in the Northwest, the differences being clouds, rain, and mud. I just couldn't imagine 'Jazz people' partying in the dust, fleas, and livestock manure.

In September on Monday morning I reported to an empty stage with an 8' x 8' workbench placed downstage. On it were plans, a tool belt, Lucky Strike and Chesterfield cigarettes, a tape measure, mechanical pencils, a couple big jars of what looked like homemade pickles and The San Francisco Chronicle. I was introduced to group of people gathering around the workbench as "a kid from Utah who's going to help with the show". The conversation immediately moved to Mormons as one of my new bosses, Al Rudis, lit up a cigar. We didn't linger on the topic and moved directly to rolling out the set design and began chatting about its execution. Someone brought a tray of coffee for all of us, which was gulped quickly. Then before I knew it some materials arrived, sawdust started flying, nails were being pounded, primer was laid and logo cutouts were being fine-tuned. It was a magic activity.

Through out the week we kept working set construction while big boxes of lights, speakers, microphones, miles of cable arrived onstage, was unpacked and set up. Electricians were climbing around the pigeon and bats nests in the rafters. Sound guys recruited everyone to help set the monster heavy consoles and lift speakers. A truck with water made laps around the arena to dampen the dust and pallets of fold out chairs were placed along the edges. Every now and then the boss, Jimmy Lyons, would do a lap in the arena and onstage smoking a Chesterfield clenching his fists and grinding a thumbnail.

Friday afternoon. We were laying the last stripes of paint when the stage manager pulled me away and said" go help that band get their stuff onstage so we can start setting up for tonight's show ". I glanced at my watch realizing curtain was in about 3 hours and paint was still being laid, lights were still being hung while the Prince of Darkness shuffled around with a cup of coffee and McCune hadn't finished checking microphones.

About 10 minutes before show time the stage manager assigned me my show station and duties which was, I had to keep my eye on the stage during the entire show in case there was an emergency. He pointed to a 2 1/2 " x 6 " slot cut in the set wall down stage left of his show lectern and said, "don't move until I tell you". Mike Wilmot then stepped over to me and spoke into my ear, "he's serious". John Lewis just raised his eyebrows. I had no idea this slot was going to be the best seat in the house for over four decades in a row.

PHOTO BY J. NICHOLS: JANET OWENS

4
J.O. – JANET OWENS 1976

41 years of jazz. Where does the time go? During those years I fell in love, married, had a family, lost a parent, lost many friends, had a number of "careers", and went to lots of different music festivals. The constant in all of that has always been the third weekend of September in Monterey.

My introduction to the festival came through Greg Floor. We'd gone to college together in Salt Lake City. Westminster College had a renowned jazz program that Greg was a part of. I really knew nothing about jazz but the band at school really knocked me out! The music was unlike anything I had ever heard. I didn't "get it"…but I knew that I loved it.

I ran into Greg one summer night the year after I graduated, 1976. We got to talking about this little jazz festival he went to in September with another college buddy, Mike Manship. Greg invited me down. He and Mike were always a lot of fun so I thought why not? My girlfriend and I loaded our sleeping bags in the back of my

VW and headed to Monterey in September.

We arrived on Friday of festival weekend, set up our camp in the stables and got ready to enjoy the 3 day party. Greg's sister Debbie manned a booth outside of the rear arena gate. Audience members could check their coolers, coats, blankets, or whatever they didn't want to take to their seats in the arena. Debbie's booth was a happening spot, there was a constant party. Since we didn't have seats in the arena we spent time in Debbie's booth and talked to everyone who came by. I'd go into the arena and sit where I could and listen to the most amazing music. Whenever I'd get up the nerve to go to the rarified air of the backstage to visit with Greg I'd be amazed by this stage crew who appeared to have everything under control in what I perceived to be chaos. Paul Vieregge looking cool, Mike Wilmot in constant motion, Greg Floor, Mike Manship, John Nichols, all getting things done. They were all hustling but such an air of camaraderie, I wanted in!

By the time that 19th annual festival was over Greg and I were seeing each other constantly and soon fell in love. Monterey Jazz became a part of our lives together. The next two years I worked as an usher during the show. The week before the festival I worked onstage helping to paint the set and getting to know the stage crew.

During the late 70s and early 80s Greg and I would travel to Monterey in our 1960 VW microbus. I always looked forward to going to Monterey. Salt Lake City summers were hot and so very dry. It was a treat to drive to the coast. Some years we would drive to LA and work our way up Highway 1. We would pull off the highway anywhere we could to just sit by the ocean. The Monterey County Fairgrounds though was always our final destination. We'd park our bus on the fairgrounds, either behind the stage or for a couple of years out in the arena. At the time there was a little caretaker cabin next to the office where we could shower, it was everything we needed. There were usually 2 or 3 vans camped out all week prior to the festival. Friday we would all move out to the stables where the concessionaires are now, and camp for the weekend. After a few years of camping, staying at the Lone Oak, and the El Castille, the festival began putting us up for the week at the Travelodge. What luxury!

Most of the crew would arrive in Big Sur on Saturday the week before the show. Paul and Penny Vieregge would host us at their home for the evening. We'd barbeque, and drink 12 year old George Dickel. "Start with the best, stay with the best" was the motto on the Dickel bottle and it suited us perfectly. We'd spend the evening catching up with each other. Even though most of us didn't see each other from one September to the next we would always take up right where we had left off the year before. We'd all camp that night at Paul and Penny's. Sunday morning we'd walk down to Pfieffer Beach. A few of us would swim in the cold Pacific to rid ourselves of the effects of the night before. Eventually we'd drive up the coast late Sunday afternoon and be ready to go to work Monday morning.

Monday we'd have the fairgrounds to ourselves. We'd sweep the stage, the backdrop would be pulled out of storage, sweep, get the walls up, sweep, tape, sweep Dutchman, sweep, and finally get ready to paint the design. Al Rudis, who was affectionately known as "the executioner" would show us the design and assign us our tasks. This was usually the first time any of us had seen the design.

Tuesday the energy on the fairgrounds would ramp up a bit with the arrival of the lights. The office staff would have arrived from Pearl Street by then. Jimmy Lyons greeted each one of us warmly, exclaiming that his "family" was all assembled and now he knew there would be a festival.

Wednesday the sound truck arrived with all of their gear and crew. The stage became a real hub of activity and very crowded. We were still painting and McCune was loading equipment onstage and Milt, the prince of darkness and his lighting crew had their boxes up there as well. Risers were being moved on and off stage so they could be swept and painted. The energy was becoming palpable on the fairgrounds.

Thursday evening after hopefully finishing the set and cleaning and prepping the stage, there would be a barbeque over in front of the garden stage area. The festival began hosting this pre-show barbeque for just the crew(s). Performers who happened to be in Monterey would join us as well. One year I remember standing by the fire carrying on with folks, swapping nonsense. There was someone next to me laughing and being as nonsensical as the rest of us. I turned and realized it was Dizzy Gillespe, relaxed and totally enjoying himself. Clark Terry came to the barbeque whenever he was in town.

I was talking to him and addressing him as Mr. Terry. He looked at me and said, "you call me CT, if you call me that I know that we're friends". I called him CT from that day on whenever he returned to the festival. Eventually we would all wander over to the arena to watch the light crew focus the lights on the set. It was wonderful to see the design we had worked on all week lit up as the audience would see it in less than 24 hours. It truly was show time.

By this time I was working full time during the show on stage. Sometime in the early 80s Paul Vieregge came to me and told me he had a change of career for me. I was going to go on the roof and work the video camera during the show. I told him I had no idea how to work a big camera like that but he said he had full confidence in my abilities. "Just point and shoot" is what he told me. The crew in the audio truck needed to be able to see what was happening on stage. A couple of the audio guys would extend a ladder to its absolute full length and send me up to the roof. I'd climb up, the ladder would then be taken away until the end of the show and when they had a free moment they would extend it again and I could come down. It would get really hot up on the roof during the day and then get quite cool during the evening show. One year, Saturday afternoon, it was very hot. I wore a skirt thinking it would help me be a bit cooler. I'd have to straddle the tripod to be able to properly work the camera. Red Hollaway was on stage. He thought I was flashing him during his set. He would be blowing that horn and just smiling up at me every chance he got. He was waiting for me when I came down the ladder. I think he was disappointed when I told him I had a pair of black shorts on under my skirt. We had a good laugh. He returned to the festival a few times after that and we continued to laugh, he'd always ask if I was going to wear my skirt again for him.

After a few years of working the camera alone Cello joined me on the roof. He put his highly technical engineering skills to work and actually tied the ladder to the roof so we could get up and down at will. The roof was such a great vantage point to see what was happening on stage as well as in the arena. There were nights of full moons or Monterey mist and always wonderful music. Soon Kasha, David, and Eric became part of the camera crew. After a few years the camera angles and the technology needed to get the shots they wanted needed to become more sophisticated. The camera was moved to its present location and more cameras were added.

A very poignant memory I have was in 1993. Greg and I had our 2 month old baby that we brought to the festival with us. I wasn't able to work as much but I wanted to be at the show with our son, one of the next generations of crew. I'd go under the stage to nurse him and let him sleep. Mike Neal would turn off the under-stage monitors and make it as quiet as he could so Will wouldn't be disturbed. Mike was so sweet about it, anything for family.

There are so many memorable moments over the years. I feel as though the performers were always so relaxed, and kicked back in Monterey. The first few years I came to the festival John Lewis was the musical director. The Modern Jazz Quartet always played the most amazing set. John Lewis was such a gentleman and seemed to go out of his way to talk to us back stage and make sure everything was ok. I remember talking to Lisa Fisher about what it was like to tour and sing with the Rolling Stones and then the pros and cons about touring with her own group. Dee Dee Bridgewater and I talked one year about our mothers who were approximately the same age and the challenges they faced living alone. Quincy Jones and I talked about Donald Trump and Hillary Clinton, both of whom he knew personally. There was a relaxed conversation with them all. Next thing you knew, they were on stage putting on an amazing performance for us all.

As I mark my 42nd year at the festival, I'm so thankful to have been a part of this group of amazing, talented, people. Although the specifics of many of the years are lost, the thing that stands out the most is the fact that the Monterey Jazz Festival stage crew, those of us who have returned year after year after year, have become my family. We all share a bond, a love, for the third weekend in September. The rest of the year we are all involved in our lives, our jobs, all over the world. But for that one week in September, we dropped it all for jazz and each other.

PHOTO BY J. NICHOLS

PHOTO BY J. NICHOLS: MIKE MANSHIP

5
MIKE MANSHIP

"He who joyfully marches in rank and file has already earned my contempt. He has been given a large brain by mistake, since for him the spinal cord would suffice." - Albert Einstein

The Monterey Jazz Festival comprises major threads in the fabric of who I am, and I know this to be true for the relationships I have made with both music and people. For twenty-seven years (then nineteen year break) and now back for three years so far. I made the pilgrimage to the golden shore from first Salt Lake City, UT, and later

West Yellowstone, MT. At first, we'd sleep backstage, and/or my Subaru parked in the arena. All new to me was creating stage sets, dressing the curtains for a clear path, performer and crew liaison, and occasional peeking through the backstage holes to view the concert, but always working inside the natural speaker that the stage itself is.

Growing up, music caught my ear but seldom held my attention. I had no background in music, and therefore lacked an appreciation for it as an art. Rock and Roll had a great feel, but I couldn't have told you which band played the radio hit, or sing you the lyrics to the song others recited in unison. All of that changed when I was able to hear Jazz at Westminster College in the early 1970's.

Two miles north of Westminster College's quaint campus lies the University of Utah. With its staggering student population, both then and now, it is easy to get lost in the mix and miss things on campus. When the Dr. Fowler and Ladd McIntosh's Jazz Department was exiled from the U of U in the early 1970's, they sought refuge at Westminster. With jazz music easily accessible at Westminster, it immediately caught my attention, and I was hooked. There were horns and keyboards in dorm rooms, clinics, and classes on campus. The musicians would also host lunch sessions in the Manford A. Shaw Building on campus. With this building being the hub of campus, it was almost impossible to escape the soulful music that was performed on campus. This was my introduction to jazz, and it couldn't have happened in a more natural, or organic way.

The Fowler Brothers, famous in the Utah Jazz Music scene helped bring the music to Westminster. Some of the artists they were able to wrangle were Frank Zappa, Canned Heat, Earth Wind and Fire, Jean Luc Ponty, Phil Woods, and many many others

Music was also brought to campus by Greg Floor on the first weekend in May, for what he termed, "Mayfest". Fitting the early seventies motto, students gathered for "one day of music and peace". Mayfest of 1974 is where I got my first taste of making stages and running equipment. When that day of work came to an end, I knew it was something I could do to be as close to the music as possible. Dr. Fowler pointed Greg to the Monterey Jazz Festival as Greg was working summer theater in Monterey. I must give thanks to Floor for this connection to jazz that brought me to California and expanded my growing appreciation for it as a music and art form. On top of that, the festival has given me the opportunity to grow, and provide me some of the best moments of my life.

I knew I was on a unique path and it felt wonderful to be able to follow a whim and experience it bloom. Paul Vieregge repeatedly inspired in us that what we were doing was significant and he taught us the importance of being entrusted with the promotion of this American art form. He would join his hands and hold them out in a cupped fashion and explain that we were holding not only the artist up, but we were conspirators in a grand spiritual enlightenment. That everyone involved had a responsibility to do their best no matter the task.

Directions on the path of life have been taught to me through working the MJF. It's a completely full circle thing. The festival needs the stage crew, our stage crew needs the musicians, the musicians need an audience, and it goes on. You can loop those scenarios however you want, but at the end of it, everyone needs each other to make the production happen. That has translated into my life away from the MJF through family, friends and work. The festival itself is very transcendent of how you treat people in real life. Respect gets respect. Disrespect does the same. No matter what you put on the line, it comes full circle in one way or another.

I have always believed Paul to be the strongest mentor in my life. Paul was a bigger than life individual, and the amount of people that feel like me is a real testament to his role in the festival for our stage crew family. Paul, along with his wife Penny, helped facilitate our crew becoming so close by hosting us at their home in Big Sur the weekend before stage construction began. Their house, nestled in Sycamore Canyon and surrounded by the large Redwood and Bay trees, made for a great relaxation spot for the crew to convene after the long year of being away. Camping on their property, we shared laughs and conversations of the year that had been. Every year upon meeting up in Big Sur, this family of ours fell right back into the groove. It never felt like we had been separated for a year, but more like a long weekend.

Big Sur served a huge role in building the chemistry between us all. For me, especially with Mike Wilmot, Paul Vieregge. The friendships that we were able to create, have further rippled through time. From very early on in his years of working the festival, Cello brought his whole family. Amazingly, Cello and his family are only some of the stage crew lineage that has become part of the festival.

Mike Wilmot already onboard at the MJF the first year I began and quickly became a great friend at the show. He could converse about anything, many interests, and he was an easy person to feel close to due to his personality. Always ready to make the best decision as needed at the moment. He and the Vieregges were some of the MJF crew that attended my wedding in Utah and that is an act I am always thankful for. Joel Wilmot, Mike's son is another second generation MJF'er who I feel close. He shares the kindred spirit his father had, and it truly amazes me how the apple rarely falls far from the tree. Joel works in theatre and stagecraft and does a great job at it.

PHOTO BY J. NICHOLS (left to right) MANSHIP, FLOOR, JOSH VIEREGGE

Josh Vieregge is another second generation MJF'er who I share a great connection with. He was able to inherit so much of his father's great qualities, but sometimes needed a change of pace, to keep going at a steady rate. He had never left California and it put him in a slump. I invited him to Utah for the winter and he carpentered and worked at Brighton Resort. I had another family-like crew of winter time athletic ski people, and knew he would fit right in. It felt special sharing that connection with one of my best friend's sons. We were able to share the connection of music and skiing, two things that I love which I believe verify me as one of the luckiest people in the world. Mary Vieregge moved to Utah as the fabric continued to be woven.

The best part about this lineage at the MJF is there are many others who got to share these similar connections to the families, including the musicians who played the shows and people of the community. These families have done great things for the festival and other music operations around the country. I feel lucky and honored to have been a part of all this beautiful history.

PHOTO BY J. NICHOLS (center) MIKE MANSHIP, MIKE WILMOT

Setting up the stages and sets, clearing way for lighting and sound set up, along with any and everything else the venue needed. This was a time when everyone got to stew in California. When applicable, some shenanigans would go down. Whether it be a little drinking, pranking or just chewing the fat and laughing up a storm. For a couple of years I would go down to the wharf and buy a large bluefin tuna. With this I would bring it back to the fairgrounds and attempt to make us all sushi. I'd go to a thrift store and get utensils. It usually tasted pretty good, though it was a hack, but more about enjoying friendship, drinks, stories, and pranks and cook in California I am no sushi chef. One year, a group of Japanese chaperones and performers came by while the infamous hacking was being prepared. Someone invited them to stay and they took us up on our offer. I could tell they were skeptical of the bearded man rolling the sushi, and after tasting, they promptly said thank you and went on their way. I always chuckle looking back on this just what Albert and I were doing may not have been quite on their level. They were incredibly polite, but it is just a story that makes me smile. Here I am, a young adult learning so many things on the fly regarding life, the festival, and, sushi!

Another thing I was able to learn on the fly during one year of the festival was mixing the sound for the house. A new sound company was hired, and they had never worked with the sounds of jazz before. They were missing the solos, recording the wrong instruments and as an overall, blowing it. Paul knew something had to be done, and he sent me out to the pit to cue to the sound company, so they could make a bearable sound for the audience. While Basie, and Gillespie and the High School band made beautiful tunes, I was tapping the sound guy on the shoulder, cueing him to turn the soloing artist up in the mix. It felt great, controlling the music in that sense. After that one year, the company was out. Paul liked my contribution and asked if would like to go help at the expanding stages and I made my way to the sound board full time for many years after that.

From all the great artists I have had the pleasure of seeing over the years, the High School and college bands that plays on Sundays continuously blows me away. These students have risen through the scholastic MJF's Jazz Competitions of California and never miss their opportunity to stun the crowd. These kids are mastering their instruments and bring happiness to so many. A highlight for me each year is in the downtime when the big bands are set is to go into the audience and sit and listen to the youth play. It always moves me emotionally. Even when thinking of many great artists I have been able to hear perform, something has always stuck out to me about the students. Listening to them build this musical masterpiece is something I think certifies I am one of the luckiest listeners alive. Lots of these players have gone on to be the next greats, which I find special as well. At such a young age finding themselves on the big stage, and later in life they find themselves back on it as an established artist/band.

Many years as an assistant on main stage I would dress the curtain as it would open and close. So, I had a little crag between the curtain and the set where I could stand on the stage invisible to all and see the universe in my ears and eyes. While that view is an ultimate pleasure, the crew is never in true relaxation mode until the day is completely over. My head would constantly be on a swivel, waiting to exchange a microphone or run something out to the stage. We were always able to do some hanging with the artists or their road crew or with each other. Milt Frankel was the Lighting Designer for many years nearly from the beginning. A soft-spoken Emmy winner with humor and homemade pickles. This was someone who I could always joke with backstage while still having my head on a swivel. He often joked with me about my dog Jonah who communicated with me via sign language, she had hearing damage. A simple "here girl" never quite worked, it always had to be a loud whistle or a good hand slap on the leg. He would ask me the signal for a bottle of whiskey or go nestle up near a pretty girl, so I could initiate conversation.

In 1983 I took a sabbatical from the festival while doing geology work. While in South Africa there was longing that I wouldn't get to see the jazz family that year, but there was no doubt in my mind that upon my return for 1984, that not a beat would be skipped. By that time, after working with the crew for nine years, the groove was well set. My return proved that. It was better than ever to see everyone, and not one beat had been skipped. Instead of it feeling like one weekend had been missed like normal years, it simply felt like I had been gone for weeks' vacation. So, after 27 years in 1997 I felt is was too much to leave home and boys behind for 10 days and decide to shut 'er down. Always when the 3rd weekend of September rolled around I would go out of my way to fill up with a bit a jazz music. Then in 2015 John Nichols got in touch with me, he was going to be a little short on stage help and asked if I could make it. Once again uncommon behaviors for the uncommon good! Remarkably you still use SM-57's SM-58' and roll a mic cord alternating back and fore and. So many of the family were still there, only 20 years older and their kids where now rockin' it. The music still acted as a joy pheromone. In so many ways it is still the same.

So, it began 43 years ago with a 19-year hiatus. It has been an uncommon path but ever so expansive. Jimmy Lyons' vision and the Festival's Board showed long game insight when they created the festival as a nonprofit educational organization. So, I continue to work as a stage assistant in 2017 as the Festival produced its 60th continuous year.

MIKE MANSHIP

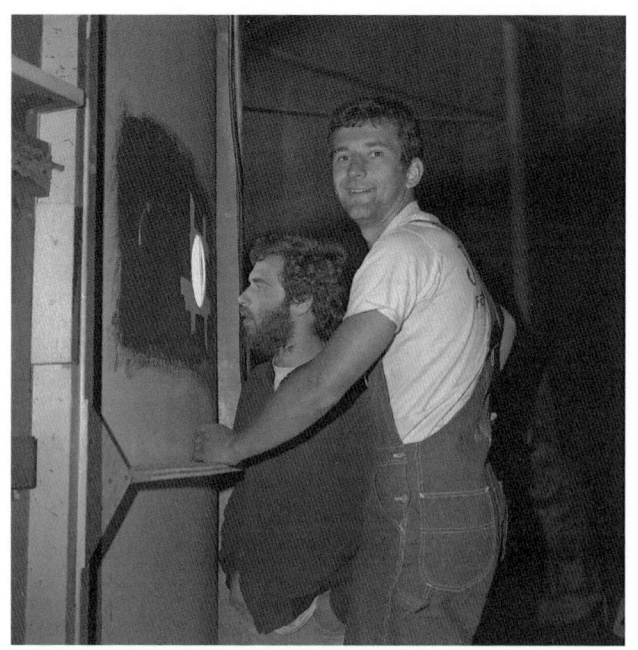

PHOTO BY J. NICHOLS: l. MIKE MANSHIP, r. CELLO

6
CELLO VITASOVIC

My first introduction to jazz music was in 1964, as a nine years old living in Zagreb, Croatia (then part of Yugoslavia). My father returned from a business trip to Germany with gifts for my sister, who was seventeen years old at the time. The gray plastic suitcase turned out to be a record player – two speakers could be detached from the sides, and lifting the lid of the middle piece would expose the turntable. Electronic gadgets were far from common in Zagreb in those days, and our family had gotten our first (small black and white) TV set a few months earlier. There was only one TV channel, and there were no programs on Tuesdays because the TV staff had a day off. The record player was an extravagant luxury; none of my sister's friends had one.

To make the gift useable, my father also purchased two 45rpm records that he chose randomly from the display. One of the records was a British band whose name I do not remember: my sister found them to be delightful. The other record was by Jonah Jones. My sister didn't care for Mr. Jones, but I did.

I played the Jonah Jones record over and over, whenever my sister was not around and I had access to the turntable. I had never heard anything like this before: happy, bouncy and mischievous. I thought that Mr. Jones was the most amazing musician in the world.

I started to search for similar music, and eventually discovered that Austria 3 radio station would play such tunes at night, starting at 11pm. This was past my bedtime, and I did not have a room of my own. I listened to this station secretly, on a small transistor radio under the covers. It was OK in the winter, but in summer time it would get quite hot – both me and the music.

Listening to the radio, I was slowly learning about jazz, and taking notes on all the interesting music that I heard, writing the names of songs and bands that I liked. Movie tickets were very cheap, so I went to the movie theater two or three time a week, and forced myself not to read the subtitles. This helped me learn English, and I could start understanding the lyrics in jazz songs as well.

I was training myself to hear the differences in tone between Ben Webster and Gene Ammonds, learning to recognize the individual voices and tones. Most of my disposable income was poured into LPs: this was my collection of magical discoveries, each album cover triggering a recollection of the moment when I heard an artist or a song for the first time... a repository of joyful surprises.

As a freshman in high school, I found out about weekly sessions dedicated to jazz in Zagreb's "Center for Culture," lead by a man called Miro Krizic. He would show up once a week, and play records from his own collection to a group of kids. It was a small room, with the capacity to seat about thirty people. In the front of the room there was a turntable, and good speakers in the corners of the room. Mr. Krizic would play his records each week to a small audience of about half a dozen regulars. He would make a brief introduction to the theme for that session (e.g. "New Orleans Piano Players" or "Early Louis Armstrong"), and then played his own LPs. He would not say much about the records, or the music. Most of the time, all of us just listened silently, and in awe.

For many people of my generation, music served as a social glue that connected boys and girls, it was an indicator of traits and interests. Your preferences in music could signal your views, your attitudes. Girls who loved the Beatles seemed more likely to choose the boys who could win approval from the girl's parents. Girls who listened to Dylan were less likely to shave their legs. Boys who loved Dylan seemed to be doing better in school. The music that I loved set me apart from these broader social circles: for the most part, I was alone when I listened to jazz. On rare occasion, I would meet a person who may have heard about Chet Baker, but very few knew about Shorty Baker.

Understanding jazz music did not always come easy to me. I read an article about Charlie Parker, and purchased one of his records. I was not prepared for the sound that came out of my speakers: it was like the record player was on the wrong speed, everything was flying so fast, my mind unable to catch up. After listening to the record for the first time, I was tired and confused. Typically, when I bought a new record, I would play it over and over until I could soak it all in, until it became soaked into my heart. I had to put this one aside for a while. I kept going back to it every few days, and after a couple of months, I started hearing the music differently. Next, I purchased the Charlie Parker With Strings album. This one won me over completely and immediately. In time, I got to love all of Charlie Parker's music, but Bird's album with strings remains my favorite because it helped me unlock a treasure.

In June of 1978 I came to America, and spent July and August working as a field laborer for a corn seed company in Kentland, Indiana. The work hours in the corn fields were long, Sun was merciless, air was humid, and the work was draining. The company employed 400 seasonal laborers from Mexico, and one boy from Croatia.

After a summer spent working in the fields, I traveled to California. By mid-September I had very little money left. I took the bus to Monterey, and walked to the office of the Monterey Jazz Festival. I had heard and read about the Monterey Jazz Festival, of course. In my eyes, it was a sacred place where all the giants mingled and made wonderful music. I did not really know what to ask for, but I also knew that only a person with authority could help me. When the office staff asked me what I want, I asked to speak to the General Manager.

A man with kind eyes and a colorful cardigan sweater came out of his office. I told him about the seed company, about the work at the farm. I talked a lot, at least for half an hour, encouraged by the patience in his eyes. Right before I left Croatia, I was briefly introduced to Bosko Petrovic, a vibraphone player who had played at Monterey. Bosko wrote a brief note on a napkin and gave it to me, suggesting that I could give the note to Jimmy Lions if I manage to find my way to Monterey. Jimmy looked at the napkin, and asked me if I would want a job. This was far more that I had expected or even dreamed.

Jimmy told me to talk to the guys backstage. Still in shock and amazed by my good fortune, I walked into the Monterey Fairgrounds. The first person I ran into was a tall bearded man with a high forehead and a receding hairline. I told him that I was looking "for the guys backstage," and Mike Wilmot said: "Well, I am one of the guys backstage." He took me to the stage, and introduced me to the rest of the crew.

I wanted to leave a good impression on the guys backstage: I could not afford to mess up this opportunity. Will they really give me a job here? Did they make a mistake? Were they actually waiting for a different lost and dirty boy from Eastern Europe, and when this real boy shows up the error will be obvious and they will fire me? As Mike and I walked towards backstage, a long list of perfectly valid reasons why they should deny me a job was rolling in front of my eyes, like the credits after a movie. I had no experience. I knew nothing about stage work. I was wearing a hat that looked like it was made of Budweiser beer labels: I paid $1.50 for it in Indiana, and it shielded me from the sun. By this time the lower part of the hat was turning brown from dried sweat and dirt. Should I take it off?

Mike was not saying much, but something about him was reassuring. He was relaxed and loose: hopefully he will be willing to tolerate my lack of any skills related to this job? He had an easy laugh and kind eyes. I certainly did not know then that Mike would become one of my closest friends, I could not imagine that we would eventually build a strong bond; however, our walk to the stage is still etched in my memory, and I felt comfortable walking in his shadow.

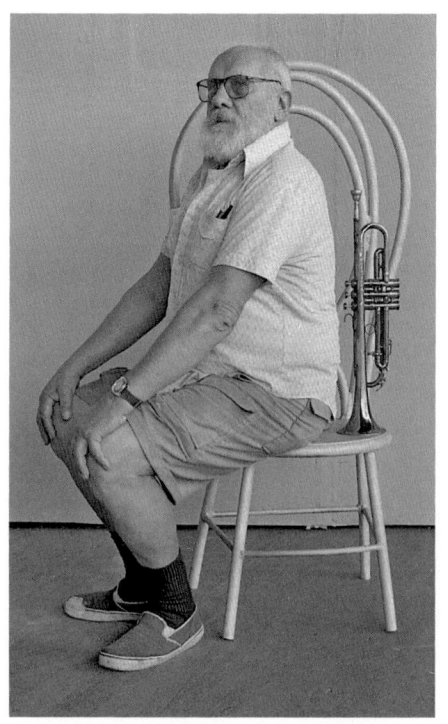

PHOTO BY J. NICHOLS: AL RUDIS

Mike introduced me to Paul Vieregge, the Stage Manager. Paul acted like it was perfectly natural for me to walk into his crew: he greeted me like he had anticipated that I would appear, he did not ask me any questions to find out what my skills were, and again I was concerned that my capable twin will appear from somewhere and burst this bubble.

Paul told me that I would be working for Al Rudis. Al was in charge of building the set, and he called himself "the Executioner" (of the stage). Al introduced me to the rest of the crew including Greg Floor, Mike Manship, Marc Meisenheimer, and Milt Frankel. It was late in the afternoon by now; they were done with the work for the day, and the cool wet air was coming onshore.

I learned that there were some food leftovers from a party in the building where "the kids" (high school band) had practiced, and was happy to find some chips and salsa there. Things would get even better: Paul said that it was OK for me to put my sleeping bag on the main stage, and sleep there. I felt like jumping from joy, but I also sensed that all the people on the crew carried themselves in a different way: I learned that the word used to describe their behavior was "cool." A "cool" person does not jump from joy: all emotions are expressed within a limited range of expressions that are greatly diminished in intensity. If you felt like a hurricane, you were to act like a breeze.

There were also opportunities to expand the vocabulary – musician was a "cat," instrument was an "ax," concert was a "gig." Being cool can be a lot of work for a foreign kid.

Stage work 101

PHOTO BY J. NICHOLS: (left to right) FLOOR, JOSH, MANSHIP, CELLO, RUDIS

Sleeping on the stage was interesting. I was thinking about all the musicians who played here… and enjoying my adventure. Used to the farm regiment and work hours, I woke up early on Tuesday morning and walked around. Some of the crew slept in their cars, parked on the fairgrounds. Al Rudis' bare feet were sticking out of the back window of his "Tin Tent" – an old VW Microbus. Mike Manship was asleep in his Subaru, laying on his back with his dog Joana curled up on his chest. Mike Wilmot and Paul had a room at the Lone Oak, and some of the crew slept on the floor there.

I went back to the stage, and was waiting to get my assignment. Around 8:30 or so, people finally started showing up on the main stage, milling around with their hands in their pockets. Paul showed up with the newspaper, found a chair, and dragged it to the part of the stage that was exposed to the morning sun. He sat down and opened up the San Francisco Chronicle. Nobody was barking any orders. Al Rudis was chomping on an unlit cigar and mumbling to himself. Greg Floor and Manship were engaged in a discussion that had too many terms from the "cool" dictionary to be coherent to an Eastern European ear. Half an hour went by, and I still had no assignments.

I was starting to worry. This seemed ominous. It was definitely not like the farm in Indiana, where white guys in pickup trucks, clad in shirts or baseball hats bearing the company logo, had no trouble finding things for me to do. I envisioned that the bubble would burst soon: this type of leisure will not be tolerated, it is too good to last... we will all get fired, and I will never work for the Monterey Jazz Festival. Some adults in charge will appear and find out that we are just "hanging out" (which apparently had nothing to do with actually hanging), and they will fire us all with righteous gusto. Timidly, I approached Paul, and stood by his chair. There must have been interesting things in the paper that day, because Paul's focus on the Chronicle did not waver. I shuffled my feet to get his attention, and asked Paul if there was anything that I should do. Paul lifted his head, looked at me over his reading glasses said, "Try smiling" and went back to reading the paper. I was entering the world of jazz.

Eventually, Al Rudis approached me and put me to work. For three next three days, I did some rudimentary carpentry, and a lot of painting. Anything that required skill was done by others, sometimes initiated by Rudis barking and mumbling but more often the experienced guys like Greg Floor would simply and smoothly slide into a new activity. Unlike me, they've been through this before.

I do not remember Paul giving orders or instructions. He just floated around, like a butterfly, seldom saying much. Sometimes he would say things that I did not understand. He would get a slight smile on his face, start a sentence in one direction, then look up, be silent for a moment, and gave me a look that seemed to say: "This is so obvious, you will not make me actually finish the sentence, will you?" I would smile back, nod, we would exchange some knowing looks, and part. I was learning to be cool. After a couple of years, I approached Mike Wilmot, and asked him about this... the eyes rolling up, Paul's sentence dissolving half way into it, and the knowing look. I said to Mike: "Sometimes I do not really understand what Paul is saying." Mike laughed, looked at me and said: "It is not a language problem. Nobody knows what Paul is saying."

PHOTO BY J. NICHOLS

In spite of the lack of any guidance or method, and without any apparent plan, the stage set somehow ended up painted and done by Thursday afternoon. We placed a small "upside down MJF chair" somewhere on the backdrop, as was the tradition at the time. When I asked Al about it, he told me that he had finished a set some years before, and they asked him "Where is the chair?" He had apparently forgotten to include a painted chair in the set, and thus added one upside-down chair on the back of the set in every subsequent year from that moment on, so that he could have an answer ready if he is ever asked that question ("Where is the chair") again (the answer being "It's there, you just have to look for it").

Al Rudis declared the stage work done, and plans were made for a celebration that evening: Thursday night was the time for the Stage Crew Party. Al Rudis drove to Fort Ord, where he obtained some food at a discount that he was entitled to as a veteran. We set up a picnic on the Fairgrounds, in front of the Garden Stage. Al Rudis moved his Tin Tent there, and pulled out his large transistor radio that included a cassette player. The crew gathered and ate, chatted, and – they drank. Bottles appeared full, and quickly became empty. Morgan was there, clicking away with her camera. Al Rudis' cassettes were playing big band music from the 20's and 30's – Fletcher Henderson, Count Basie.

The Stage Crew Party was an intimate and wonderful affair in those early days. The crew paid for the food, but we also owned the party. Sometimes musicians would stop by and chat with us: I specifically remember meeting Clark Terry there. Until then, I thought he was just a face on coveted album covers.

PHOTO BY J. NICHOLS: CELLO, PENNY VIEREGGE, MANSHIP

After the food was gone and the last remnants of sunshine were gone from the sky, the crew walked over to the Main Stage to watch the electricians test the lights. Thursday night would be the first opportunity for the stage crew to see the stage illuminated. Milt Frankel, the Prince of Darkness, would be testing the lights. Milt was a sweet man who brought his homemade pickles to the festival, where he shared them with the crew. He also had a note from his wife stating that Milton has her permission to do whatever he wants during the Festival.

I sat with the crew in the seats that had just been set up for the patrons, checking out the stage set. I was soaking up the banter and the laughter of the stage crew, not quite ready to join in. Being happy came so easily to these people, but I was still holding on to my Easter European stiffness and shyness. Josh and Mary Vieregge, Paul's son and daughter, also showed up: both of them young and hip. Janet Owens was there, with blond hair, a bottle in her hand, and a big, open laugh.

It was a truly beautiful evening, and a glorious feeling. I was part of the crew now. Really? Can this be possible?

During that 1978 show, my job was to carry the gear up the stairs to the stage, and to move it around as directed by Mike Wilmot or Greg Floor. I was a slow learner, partly because there was a general reluctance by everybody on the crew to define, structure, document, or explain anything that had to be done. There was little advanced planning. Events were expected to be handled as they happen. Everybody was supposed to know what to do, and it was all supposed to somehow come natural to us. I was studying Engineering at that time, and had already developed an engineering mind. Working without a structure made me sweat.

My work was mostly done between the sets, so I was able to watch the show from backstage, through the small round holes in the backdrop. They were intended mostly for photographers, and it was considered bad form to spend too much time at a specific hole. I moved around, looked for ways to see the stage without upsetting anybody.

I was watching Dexter Gordon's set when he turned around, walked towards my hole, and blew a couple of bars directly at me, from a few feet away. His eyes were rolled back. It felt like I was struck by lightning. He turned around to face towards the audience again, and walked away from the backdrop. It took me a while to recover from the shock.

Once the show started, I met some of the people who worked in the front office: including David Murray, Terry Cox, and Darlene Chan. I didn't know then that I would become friends with all these wonderful people. I didn't know if I would every see them again.

It was difficult for me to comprehend that I was suddenly surrounded by real people who were behind those LP covers that I had been so meticulously caring for in my small room in Zagreb; music on those records was so different from my reality in Zagreb that I came to believe that the musicians inhabit some other world, a world not accessible to me.

And then Dizzy showed up: a huge presence, a powerful sound, a giant.

I was trying to remember every moment of the festival, hear every note the musicians played, soak it all in and keep it forever. It made me incredulous and angry when I saw people in the audience chatting, laughing, socializing while the music was playing. Didn't they realize that Kenny Burrell is on stage? What could be more interesting, more important than that? Every night, after we cleaned up the stage, I put my sleeping down on the main stage and thought about all the marvelous things that happened that day. Yes, Dizzy had just been there a few hours ago, he blew his bent horn right there, a few feet away from where my sleeping bag was now. Dexter Gordon rolled his eyes at me standing right over there, in that spot. I was part of this story now. I was in the right place, at the right time.

After the last show on Sunday, and after we cleaned everything up, we went to the office to collect the leftover programs. Jimmy Lyons gave me an inscribed copy of his book, and also had some nice spoken words for me. The man in the cardigan acted like a friend. The voice from the Concert by the Sea album was now speaking to me. My idols and heroes were his personal friends.

I had a few days left before my flight back to Zagreb, and less than $50 in my pocket. Mike Wilmot came to my rescue, and offered that I could stay with him for a few days. But first, we would go to

Big Sur and spend time in Paul's house.

A small group of us went down to Big Sur on Monday, including the amazing Darlene Chan. There was a party on Monday night, and lots of drinking. The festival was officially over, but these folks were clearly still festive. I slept on a bench that was on the porch: that would become the place where I would end up spending many nights in the following years, before or after the Festival. I claimed one half, and Mike Wilmot the other half.

On Tuesday morning, while those who partied more intensely the night before were still asleep, the early risers including Darlene Chan, Tony Molina and I took a walk from Paul's cabin down to Pfeiffer Beach. When she worked, Darlene had the intensity of a four-alarm fire combined with the focus of a laser beam. From her small frame, she projected unquestionable authority and full competence. Well-hidden underneath all that steel, there was a kind and compassionate heart. In private conversations she was thoughtful, guarded and careful. It was a bright sunny morning on Pfeiffer Beach, with waves crashing on the rocks. Tony wanted his photo taken as he was standing on a rock, and as I was setting up the shot a large wave almost knocked him off the rock. I chose to have my photo taken as I stood safely on the sand.

If I was to sum up my first Jazz Festival, it would come to three things. I saw my jazz heroes live and up close. I found them to be interesting human beings, not just fantasies based on LP covers. I met people who would eventually become my closest and dearest friends. Jimmy Lyons gave me more than a job: I was adopted into a family.

Back in Croatia, I had a couple of friends who were interested in jazz. I enjoyed talking to them, but I had never met somebody like Mike Wilmot or Darlene Chan before. Mike not only knew of Fletcher Henderson and his band: he also had interesting things to say about it. Sometimes people liked jazz for the wrong reason: perhaps it would make them look more sophisticated or interesting? Mike and Darlene loved jazz for the right reasons. I could talk to Mike about things that really mattered to me. He was curious and well read. Mike had an easy way about him, and being around him I felt light and free. By that time in my life, I had built special filters to manage my communication with the outside world: when I met somebody, I would first try to find out a bit about them, to better understand which filter to apply. Each filter excluded a certain topic: depending on my interlocutor, I would employ specific filters to screen out religion, jazz, opera, poetry... but with Mike, I could toss these filters aside.

Mike lived in a very small house on Bonita Street. To say that the house was small is an understatement: it was a tiny, one bedroom place. I slept on the floor, of course. One morning a bunch of kids burst in through the front door and ran through the house... Mike's son Joel was the youngest and the slowest in the group.

Mike was betting on football games, so on Sunday he turned on a very small TV in this tiny house to follow the games. The reception was not the best, but most of the time one could at least get the sound; however, when it came time to report the results for all the games, the picture and sound would disappear and there was just static. Mike would start slapping the TV set, and it would of course recover just in time for Mike to clearly hear the commercials.

In 1979, I managed to come back from Croatia to Monterey for the jazz festival. None of the crew knew that I would be coming. I had just graduated from University of Zagreb, and received my degree in Mechanical Engineering. I was scheduled to start the mandatory service in Yugoslav National Army in December of that year.

Wearing my worn-out Budweiser hat again, I walked into the fairgrounds unannounced. This time, I easily found the crew. It was good to see the surprise on their faces, although I must say that Paul was not really surprised; he acted like he had expected to see me again - a lot of hugging, California style, but quite real. I was a bit less confused than the first time, and not quite so clueless.

The first festival seemed like an incredible adventure, unreal, fantastical, like a dream. This second one felt like a family reunion. The first year, I was in shock the whole time. The second year, I could start relaxing and developing friendships.

I developed a great fondness for Al Rudis. Underneath the rough exterior, there was a heart of gold. After the Festival, I spent a few days at his place on the West side of San Francisco. I would wonder around the City, go to Berkeley, and look for record stores. One time Al's son Alex went with me, but he refused to enter Tower Records "because they put Aretha Franklin into the jazz section." Alex was trying to get his start as a musician, and told me that he would soon have a gig playing for deaf people. When he saw the look on my face, he explained that they are not completely deaf, and that they enjoy feeling the vibration. I think they had to play loud for that crowd.

After wondering around town, I would come to Al's place in the evening, and he would tell me about his young days in Chicago, where he attended the Chicago Art Institute. Al had also worked at KGO for a while, with Paul and Mike Wilmot. One night I found Al sitting in the kitchen, with his fat white feet in a vibrating plastic tub filled with water, clad in his bathrobe, reading the newspaper, and smoking a cigar. He had just purchased the massage gizmo. We would listen to his cassettes and talk about jazz and politics. I got a sense that Al came from a family that had been quite prominent in Lithuania.

One day during that visit, I went to hear the Count Basie band at the Great American Music Hall. Since I had to rely on public transportation and was not very familiar with San Francisco, I arrived late, just before the show was about to start. The man at the door told me that they were full. I almost broke down crying, and begged him to let me in. He took pity on me, and gave me a seat in the first row – sharing a table with a beautiful black woman. She was kind enough to let me sit at her table. I noticed that she was exchanging glances with Freddy Green the whole time.

Listening to the Basie band from the front row was like sitting in front of a train – the rhythm section was tight, the horns in sync, and the smiling sea lion sitting at the piano would toss in a few "plink plink" notes to move this marvelous and powerful machine in a different direction. I thought that the night could not possibly get better, but then Carmen McRae came out to sing, standing just a few feet from me. I was shaking in my seat and sweating, definitely failing in attempts to act cool.

BACKSTAGE

PHOTO BY SUZKA: MORGAN

In the years to come, I also got to know a bit more about Bob Morgan, who looked like he came out of a Woody Guthrie biopic cast: a quiet person who did nice things for other people and always had candy for kids.

When Luka and Mima were kids, for many years they benefited from Bob Morgan's generosity, and his habit to bring candy backstage and dispense it to the kids. Years later, I asked Bob to take a photo with Luka and me. The following year, this most modest and decent man cut this photo to create two separately framed photos (one of me and one of Luka), and he gave them to us as gifts. He did not realize that for Luka and me, Bob Morgan was the most valuable part of the photo.

I also got closer to Mike Manship, whom everybody called "Docter" and he spelled it "Docter." We were making plans to go to South America together, and he promised that this would be a great adventure.

The music was great again at the 1979 Festival. Dizzy's horn would puncture the night sky again, and Woody Herman led his herd, stampeding through standards. Stan Getz, of course, with that wonderful, seductive tone.

I came back to Croatia from the 1979 Festival at the end of September, and married Marina in Zagreb about a week later. In December 1979, I reported for duty to the Yugoslav National Army.

I was not allowed to receive foreign mail while in military service, so Marina brought me letters from Mike Wilmot and passed them on to me when she came to visit. Only two people sent me letters while I was in the service, and Mike Wilmot was one of them. I had a terrible time in the military, and Mike's letters brought me in touch with another world; they were a source of hope, a connection to the world I wanted to belong to. I am glad that I have told Mike several times how much those letters meant to me, so he could not leave us without being aware of this.

I was stationed in Ljubljana, and that winter was cold and wet as usual. They would roust us out of our bunks around 4:45am, and by 5am we had to be lined up downstairs for inspection. This was a wonderful chance for the officers to purge all the aggression out of their system, yelling about meaningless infractions that we were committing so early in the day. Usually there would be military announcements on the PA system, but one day the officer in charge of the PA must have been delayed, so they just let the radio program play through the PA system for a couple of minutes.

So, that morning I heard a couple of minutes of Duke Ellington's big band playing *Things Ain't What They Used To Be* over the PA system. Johnny Hodges was by that time already one of my favorite musicians, the king of tone. That sound will put a smile on your face even if you are cold and miserable, wearing clothes intended to make you look like all the other pitiful bastards around you. I felt ten feet tall.

Because of the obligatory engagement in the Yugoslav National Army, I missed the 1980 Festival. I would be back in 1981, however, and every year since then.

My son, Luka was born in March of 1980, while I was in the service. I got out of the Army in November of 1980, and left for the US within two weeks after being discharged from service. I had a full scholarship to attend a Ph.D. program in the US. Marina, Luka and I arrived to Houston Texas in December of 1980. At the airport, I looked at the Yellow Pages and booked us into a room at a hotel that had the word "University" in its name. Our welcoming party consisted of immigration officials who carefully checked our visas. Luka was eight months old, and Marina was pregnant again with our daughter Mirna (Mima).

After a couple of months, Marina went back to Croatia to give birth there, because we did not have health insurance in the US and pregnancy was a "pre-existing condition." I bought a used 1963 Chevy Biscayne from an old lady, studied 14 hours per day, and took jobs with different professors to stay financially afloat.

Mima was born in July 1981, and the family joined me in Houston that August. Luka was 18 months old when our family finally had a chance to live together. In September of that year, I drove the '63 Chevy to Monterey, leaving the young family at home. This was the first year for me to attend the party at Paul's place, held on a Saturday a week before the Festival. I reclaimed the spot on the bench on his porch as my sleeping spot. I shared that bench with Mike Wilmot for many years. Most of the others slept in their cars. I woke up early as usual, and Penny was up soon as well. We sat in front of the fireplace in their cabin, and we spoke quietly while others were sleeping around us. This too became a tradition: for many years that followed, Penny and I would have our morning talk whenever I visited.

Penny would start the fire, and the cabin would warm up a bit. Just like talking to Paul, a conversation with Penny would include moments when I did not quite know what exactly we were talking about. In those moments, Penny's body language was certainly different from Paul's: while Paul would open up his arms, turn his palms up, tilt back his head, and roll his eyes upward, Penny would look straight at me, and often laugh. In all of these cases, I did not want to let them know that I was lost, because I did not want to break that thread that connected us. So, what if I did not quite understand? The fireplace was getting hot, the feeling was getting warmer, and we will eventually reconnect to some topic that I can understand. Why worry about details?

Penny could talk about anything, she spoke candidly, and would show interest even in dry subjects connected with my engineering work. She had a child's curiosity combined with an adventurous mind, in perpetual exploration mode. After my divorce and during my days as a single man, she patiently listened to reports about my state of mind, and generously shared advice about potential partners. Several years after my divorce, on the porch of her cabin, Penny performed the ceremony for my second wedding. My first wedding included just two close friends who served as witnesses and no family or guests; for the second wedding I scaled things down, so Penny asked her neighbor to come over and serve as a witness.

The music program in 1981 was, again, wonderful. I saw more faces from album covers. I found out that Mike Manship, the Docter, went to South America without me. Son of a bitch. I called him a few days ago, to tell him that he should get busy writing his story for this book. He asked me not to complain about him going to South America without me, and of course I had to tell. I've been giving him a hard time about this for almost 40 years, so why stop now?

The first several years, I worked the main stage. Sometime in the early 1980s, they started the Garden Stage. The first, year, I recall that the program was short and included mostly street performers, musicians and jugglers. John Nichols managed it, and after a couple of years the program grew substantially. Mike Wilmot dispatched me there, to help out. This gave me a chance to spend a bit of time with Jim, Leslie, and Albert. Joel Wilmot also worked there for a while.

During those years, the Blues afternoon show on Saturday, was managed by Mark Naftalin. Since Jimmy Lyons didn't care about blues so much, he preferred to delegate that portion of the show. The backstage area on Garden Stage is small, so I had a chance to interact with many of the artists. Many of the musicians would arrive on a buss (the Stage Crew called it "The Blues Buss from Hell") that would discharge them on the lawn behind the stage. It was hard to tell musicians from their friends and family members, as they all poured out together, in a jovial mood and ready for the festivities.

There was so much to learn there: about blues music, about the people who made it and played it, and about my fellow crew members; Jim Merical, kind and smart, so apparently in love with Leslie. Leslie: easy going but responsible, caring and open.

Manship worked the sound at the Garden Stage during those years, and Jeremy was there as well. They were later replaced by McCune professionals – which I felt was like replacing family members with professionals: they might do a better technical job, but something of great value and seemingly intangible, may be eroded.

In 1979, I slept on the Garden Stage (hard cement floor), and then later David Murray allowed Manship and me to crash in the office (when it was on Fremont street) after the office staff left for the day. We could not believe the luxury: the floor was carpeted!

In 1983, I brought Marina, Luka, and Mima to their first festival. We drove from Houston, TX to Monterey in the '63 Biscayne: no air conditioning, metal dashboard frame, two kids in diapers in the back seat. It's early September, all of us sweating and sticking to the vinyl seats. We came to Paul's party first, where my family met the crew for the first time. The first person they encountered was Morgan, who approached as I was parking the car. Then came all the other crew members, reassuring my family with hugs and smiles. Living in Houston, far away from any blood relatives, Luka and Mima started realizing that there was this strange extended family out here in California, a group of people who did not look like us, did not act like people they had met in Texas, and who acted as family.

I completed my Ph.D. at Rice University (Environmental Engineering) in 1985, and moved to Seattle. Travel to Monterey morphed into family car trips, from Seattle. The '63 Chevy was succeeded by a tiny Toyota Tercel station wagon. Mima and Luka eventually started working on the stage, and became full-fledged crew members. After the festival was over, around 3am on Monday, the family would pile into the car, I would get a large coffee to go from Denny's, and drive to Seattle without stopping except for bathroom breaks and gas.

I experienced some magic moments on the Garden Stage: Mima and Luka on stage, singing along with Rockin' Sydney on Don't Mess with My Toot Toot, Katy Webster proving the appropriateness of her middle name (Jewel), Dottie Ivory turning her back side to the audience and doing her "butt dance" to the great delight of the screaming patrons. Also, memories of conversations with Albert when he was discouraged and contemplating whether he should return to the Festival after he had been treated unfairly. Observing Joel Wilmot maturing from a Northern California boy into a sensitive, intelligent young man. Talking to Jim Merical about his work, geek to geek.

After a few years at the Garden Stage, Mike asked me to help out Janet, who was operating the camera on the roof above the bleachers. Janet and I would frame a single wide shot at the beginning of an act, and make sure that all the musicians are included. The camera feed served the radio guys in the truck parked below: this allowed them to see the stage as they were doing the live show inside the truck. So, Janet and I were basically the video crew for a radio show.

It was a wonderful gig for Janet and me: we had the best seats in the house, and time to hang out. We brought up sleeping bags to keep us dry from the wall of cool moisture that would envelop us each evening, packed enough hot cocoa in the thermos to keep us warm, and had plenty of music to keep us happy.

Part of our job was to keep the inebriated fans from using our ladder and climbing up on the roof, thus adding safety and security to our list of responsibilities. Jane occasionally provided inspiration for the performing artists: however, this is a story that she should tell.

As we shared the hot cocoa on the roof, Janet and I gradually developed a strong bond as friends. I did my best to make her laugh, because when Janet laughs the stage lights come on. And whenever she did laugh, I knew that I had to make that happen again. It was like shooting a cannon and then observing an avalanche, and enjoying the view of all of its power.

Jimmy Lyons retired at his 35th festival. I spoke to him then, and although he said no bitter words, I was crushed by the sadness in his eyes. I love Errol Garner's music, but sometimes I put on Concert by the Sea just to hear Jimmy's voice in the beginning of the album.

After Jimmy's era was brought to a close, I was introduced to two people: Tim Jackson and Susan (Suzka) Collins. I was quite anxious about the transition from Jimmy to a new manager, because Jimmy had such a personal impact on the Festival. The festival reflected his personality: I was afraid that everything could change.

After 25 years of working under Tim, I must say that I cannot imagine anybody else who could be so kind to the legacy of Jimmy Lyons, so understanding of the intangible spirit of the Festival, so respectful to the traditions, and still open enough to allow the Festival to grow and change. (I will let Suzka explain how she became involved in the Monterey Jazz Festival: it is one of my favorite MJF stories.)

Suzka brought new ideas, and made changes. Executing the set no longer included only stage crew painting with brushes: there were large canvasses that Suzka had prepared in her studio before the Festival, with an intention to hang them in front of the backdrop. Sometimes she would construct strange painted structures: in one case, such a structure was immediately nicknamed "a floating dick," but hey, she is an artist, and it all served its festive purposes.

Suzka moved to California from Chicago. One time in those early years, I asked her what she misses most from Chicago, and she told me that she had just ordered a sandwich from her favorite deli there: she asked them to send it to her via FedEx.

After she had completed the implementation of her first set, Suzka and I stood in the audience and looked at the stage. Suzka asked me what I thought, and I told her that "this is not going to work." Of course, after her design was revealed to everybody, there was much talk about the wonderful new stage design. As I was hearing this, an image would pop up in my mind: a grizzled old curmudgeon sitting in a chair, reading the paper, and soaking his tired feet in a tub of warm and vibrating water; was I turning into Al Rudis? No, it could not be: in addition to being a curmudgeon, Al Rudis was also an educated and talented artist. I had only learned the curmudgeon part from Al Rudis.

Last year, when I moved into a newly purchased house, Suzka drove up from San Diego to Redondo Beach, and gave me a piece of art to a prime slot on my pathetically empty walls: a piece of a large canvass that was originally part of that MJF set design. This time, I could clearly see that it would work beautifully. When I look at this canvass in my living room, I feel the warmth of her friendship, and I can almost hear the music.

In addition to different ideas about the stage designs, Suzka also brought great positive energy to the crew. Suzka treated her painting crew with love and encouragement. She took Mima under her wing, treated her with love and respect, and made her feel comfortable.

The year of this writing is 2017, and I hope to work as member of the Monterey Jazz Festival Stage Crew next September for the 39th time. As I look back, I remember many situations, events, and people… but it is difficult to place them accurately into a chronological order. Since I have not kept a diary, and also failed to properly organize records and photographs, today I can only access my memories through the imperfect vehicles of recollection… as I collected these images and sounds through the years, my brain has dropped the slide tray a few times, the memories spilled out onto a disorganized pile, and I can no longer restore the original order…

During each festival, the Stage Crew had opportunities to spend time together as friends. This "hanging out" included different parties. This would start on a Saturday before the Festival weekend, with a barbecue at the Vieregge place in Big Sur. On Sunday morning, I would have my early morning talk with Penny and a walk to the beach… and by the time I was back from the beach, the rest of the crew would be waking up. We would all drive up to Monterey, and usually split into two groups: most of the guys would watch football, usually in Mike Wilmot's room.

During the week, our modest Thursday night Stage Crew Party gradually grew in size and in the number of attendees: it became an official MJF event. In the early days, Morgan would bring the slides from the previous festival, and project them on the. She used to record everything that was done, in the background, to transform the Monterey Fairgrounds into the site of the Monterey Jazz Festival. Her slides included all the stages of this transformation and featured crew members. In later years, the Thursday Night Barbecue gradually morphed into even more formal, catered event that includes many guests and a band performance. The Garden Stage crew would work.

This encouraged us to move "our" party to a different day. For several years, every Stage Crew member had to show up with slides and make a presentation (on Wednesday night) about his/her life during the remaining 51 weeks of the year. This morphed into an opportunity for the audience to make fun of the presenter. While the presenter designated for that year was preparing their slides, others were secretly planning the coordinated heckling: e.g. whenever Buddy Chew would utter the word "Mammoth" (he had recently moved to Mammoth Lakes), we would jump up and do our impersonations of the wooly mammoth; whenever he would say the word "snow," we would throw marshmallows at him.

An important lesson that I have learned from Paul Vieregge's management style is that the order or structure are not the most important. Paul did not even provide inspiration by projecting his vision on you: in his quiet way, he simply awoke the love and passion that each one of his crew members already carried inside. He was a conductor without a baton, a herder without a whip.

Paul did not select his crew based on their skills and experience related to stage work. Actually, he did not care at all about your stage work experience. He cared about your life experience, and he wanted to know why you are there. Our job was not to paint and move gear: he wanted us to care. He figured that if we care, if we are there because we love the festival and the music, we could easily learn how to paint.

I do not know any crew members who came to the Festival based on financial analysis. I was first paid ($100) in 1981, and Mike Wilmot later gradually increased it to the point where I can break even with my expenses. However, I feel that I have received enormous value from working as a crew member since my first day there. It is a life-long educational program for me, and I feel that being a crew member made me a better person.

Each festival added to my collection of "most valuable personal moments" that could be recalled later, and also lessons that could be applied to the remaining 51 weeks per year of my life. Some of the old traditions are now gone, and some new ones have emerged. Some of my friends have passed on: I can no longer call Mike Wilmot after I finish reading a new book, or after I've heard some artist that I had not known about. I cannot talk to Al Rudis and learn about his adventures as a young man. I cannot drive up to Big Sur in October to jointly celebrate our birthday with Paul (we were born on the same date).

PHOTO BY J. NICHOLS: VIEREGGE CABIN, BIG SUR

About three weeks before Paul passed on, I drove up to Big Sur to see him. He was a bit weak by then, in hospice care. I asked Paul something that I had always been curious about: who was his favorite musician? He said it was Ben Webster. When I got back to LA, I went to the Amoeba record store and bought a double album featuring Ben Webster and Johnny Hodges: Hodges is my favorite musician. I sent the album to Paul, and Penny later told me that he loved it, and played it many times during those last weeks. This means the world to me.

After Paul passed away, there was a wake at the Big Sur cabin. Most of the stage crew was there, and each person brought a small item to lay down next to the urn with Paul's ashes, to be buried in the yard. I brought my Budweiser hat, since it helped me get into a place that accepted me. Penny and I had one of our morning talks the next day, when this photo was taken.

MJF gave me a chance to meet some wonderful people. My encounters with artists and jazz people whom I have revered, people like Jimmy Lyons, John Lewis, James Moody, Etta James, and so many others, were very brief and certainly not memorable to them. However, they were of great importance to me. I tried to learn from their music, from their behavior. If I am trying to act like a gentleman, I think: how would John Lewis behave in a situation like this?

When I am managing people, I recall the lessons that Paul taught me: people are inspired by love, and they will find a way to get the work done if you give them your trust. And, importantly, work can be fun.

When I listen to some new jazz, I often recall my conversations with Mike Wilmot. Sometimes we disagreed: I was offended when he said that Louis Prima was a clown. Mike did not care much for Tom Waits. I adore both artists. However, Mike taught me that I am not the only person who cares about this music. As my initial rooftop camera gig gradually grew into a professional video shoot with multiple cameras and a director,

PHOTO BY J. NICHOLS

PHOTO BY J. NICHOLS: LUKA VITASOVIC

7

LUKA VITASOVIC 1983

One of my earliest memories of the jazz festival was, fittingly, not of the festival itself, but of the family road trip to get there. I say fitting because these road trips would become folded into the tradition of these outings as much as anything else, often possessing the magical combination of my dad driving for implausible stretches of time and my sister and I getting antsy in the backseat. Inevitably this would lead to me antagonizing my sister, and some squabble breaking out as my dad hit hour eighteen behind the wheel as he was nearing his breaking point.

During my early years at the festival, my eastern European parents had settled on a suburb of Houston, Texas for their initial foray into living in America. Being that we were now living in the good ol' U.S. of A, the obligatory mode of transportation was an American classic car. The classic car of choice (or financial necessity) for my father was a 1963 Chevy Biscayne sedan. It came complete with the hot weather package of no A/C, plastic covered seats, and a metal steering wheel and trim. This ensured a steering wheel too hot to initially grasp and seats that heated up quite efficiently after sitting out in the hot Texas sun.

Bouncing along in our '63 Chevy through the southwest United States on our way to Monterey, I pitched my parents on the idea of playing an innocuous sounding game I invented called 'butterfly'. At this point, we were hours into driving through one of the many desert-like terrains during our voyage. They probably recognized that the thought of me entertaining myself quietly and innocently in the backseat was a mirage, but the allure of quiet relief from my antics proved too much, and without hesitation my proposal was quickly approved.

Dust sprayed everywhere as our car slowed from 85 MPH and quickly found respite on the side of the road. I was inconsolable in the back seat and my parents frantically tried to figure out what went wrong. As it turns out, 'butterfly' is where a small toddler holds their favorite shoe out of the window of a very fast moving vehicle to see if it flies. What I quickly learned is that I wasn't strong enough to hold on to the shoe and it went flying out of my hand and off the side of the road.

After many treks across the southwest United States we eventually moved out to Seattle, WA and that served as the new starting point for our adventures. These drives would often include repeated questions of "are we there yet?", please to stop the vehicle *immediately* because there was a restroom emergency, and eventual naps in the backseat. All of this occurred to a vibrant soundtrack of Louis Prima bellowing about Pennies from Heaven or Johnny Hodges effortlessly winding his way through one of his masterful solos.

We would be in that car for what seemed like a lifetime, cramped in the back of a compact economy car itching for our final destination. All those feelings of claustrophobia, restlessness and motion sickness would soon be wiped out with a single, solitary sight. The Pacific Coast Highway does not need any help or require any assistance in standing out as a scenic marvel. Somehow, that gorgeous stretch of road managed to take on an amplified beauty one wouldn't think was possible. And yet it was. For that winding ocean front road carved between the Cypress trees and the ocean, nestled amongst the cliffs in a truly serene manner meant we were close, and that our destination was within grasp.

The destination was Big Sur, the home of Paul and Penny Vieregge. Penny is one of the kindest people you will ever meet. I am convinced that her warmth served as a homing beacon that successfully guided all the crew to their house for the annual pre-festival get together. For many years Paul was the stage manager for the main stage of the festival. He had worked that stage back when Jimmy Hendrix was gesticulating in front of a packed crowd with a guitar and lighter fluid at the Monterey Pop Festival. But to me, he was Paul. Paul was the epitome of a cool customer; always chill, as unflappable as they come. Even at a young age I managed to derive a secret pleasure watching my father and Paul interact.

If you took Woody Allen's character in Annie Hall and somehow combined it with Robert DeNiro, you would end up with a fair approximation of my father. A neurotic, constantly worrying immigrant who likes to use hand gestures that give off the impression to an onlooker that this man is either describing the best pasta Bolognese he's ever had or doling out an order to whack somebody. He wasn't always that way; he used to be quite care free, skip class, and engage in all kinds of shenanigans with his friends growing up. But moving to another country with a small child, a pregnant wife, and two suitcases will cause you to come face to face with reality. While studying at Rice University in Houston, he would stay up for days on end working hard until he would collapse and sleep for 24 hours straight. No matter how successful he would become with his work, no matter how stable his job would be, this sense of worry, this sense of weight, would never leave him.

While these feelings would never go away for my father, one week out of every year they would dissipate. Coming off a 900-mile drive, he would lumber out of the car and make his way up to the Vieregge home. The contrast in demeanor between Paul and my father could not be more stark. Paul took laid back to a level few thought was attainable. My joy came from watching Paul greet my father and, in the most unassuming manner, melt away the baggage and stress he'd been carrying. Sometimes all it took was Paul's smile and a nod, but it always brought me a profound sense of happiness to see my dad at peace like that.

A short walk from the Vieregges' place, a group of us ventured down to a picturesque cove to enjoy the walk, the company, and the gorgeous setting that awaits. Little did I know what was REALLY in store! One…..two….. THREE! The salty tang of the ocean filled my nose as I worked to gain my bearings, submerged in the waters of Pfeiffer Beach. The culprits of how I ended up submerged amongst the waves are one Joel Wilmot and Josh Vieregge. Being the generation ahead of me at the festival they were young, cool, ultra-hip giants that I looked up to with awe. That's why Joel was able to grab my arms, and Josh my feet, and toss me into the ocean on that Saturday afternoon. That's why when I was roughly seven years old and Joel was seventeen, I offered little resistance as he and Josh stapled me to the stage by my baggy overalls. I just wanted to belong and to be able to call these guys my friends.

I can still remember when I got the news that I could finally help Josh out in the Nightclub during the actual festival. I was in heaven. I got to pal around with Josh all day, work in the nightclub, and be one of the boys. I had made it! My main task that year was to correctly plug in all of the microphone cables during the set change. With my level of excitement and sense of belonging you would have thought I had been tasked with looking after the country's nuclear codes.

That's the thing about experiencing something starting at the age of two years old. Your experience is filtered through the lens of what stands out to you at that time. For many of my years at the festival, I was a kid. What stood out for me at age six was getting candy from the ever reliable Bob Morgan. At age eight it was going to the famous Monterey Bay Aquarium. What stood out for me at age fourteen was volunteering to transport anything I could think of between stages, because then I got to drive the golf carts. What I am incredibly thankful for is that my love, my appreciation, and my awareness of the music managed to be captured in that filter and didn't get lost in all of my juvenile distractions.

How could it get lost when you're surrounded by the likes of Ray Brown, John Lee Hooker, and Dee Dee Bridgewater as a kid? I still remember the goose bumps I got while being mesmerized by Gene Harris and his incomparable rendition of Summertime; or Dizzy Gillespie pulling my leg and giving me a hard time that I was running around backstage asking everyone else for their autograph first before finally asking him.

When you grow up watching Etta James making crass gestures to a heat and booze-fueled blues afternoon crowd, while bellowing a devastating tale about how she'd rather go blind than watch her lover leave, that gets burned into your memory. There's no getting away from that. I mean that in the best possible way. If that doesn't leave a mark, then you have no pulse.

These shows also went well beyond the music. I have pictures stored at my mom's house of Etta James bouncing my sister and I on her knee backstage. When I was around eight years old, her then sax player, Red Holloway, came up and asked me if I played an instrument. I told him I played piano and he gently teased me that the two times a week I was practicing wasn't going to cut it. The next year, in a truly unforgettable moment, Red saw me backstage and asked me how the piano practicing was coming along.

It is these experiences that truly make the Monterey Jazz Festival so special. Not only does the sense of family extend to the stage crew and all of the people that make the festival possible, but it extends to the artists. As I have the blessed fortune of now getting to bring my young daughter to the Festival and hopefully carry on this tradition, I am forever grateful for the music, experiences, and people that have given me a second home and a lifetime of memories. To see my now six year old daughter dancing to Davina and the Vagabonds at the same Garden Stage where more than twenty years ago I sang "Don't Mess with my Toot Toot" on stage with Rockin' Sidney brings me immeasurable joy.

BACKSTAGE

PHOTO BY J. NICHOLS: THE GARDEN STAGE

] GARDEN STAGE OPENED IN 1983 [

PHOTO BY TOM COPI: JOHN NICHOLS, JASON SLATE, BUDDY CHEW

8

Taken from John Nichols' written notes

By 1983 I had quit teaching and could became a full time member of the crew. On Monday night Paul Vieregge talked to me at the football party in his motel room. He told me that the festival had sold out the main arena again and it had been decided to add two more stages for music and sell grounds passes for $10 for people who could not get into the main arena. It was not called the Jimmy Lyons Stage at this time. He asked me if I wanted to become stage manager of the outdoor stage. I was thrilled, honored, gratified, and probably a little nervous. I said yes. I later walked over to the drug store and bought a clip board, some paper and pens and pencils. Then I started thinking about someone to work on the crew with me. Jason Slate was going to run the sound board. I was going to run the stage. I needed an extra stage hand.

I had a multi-talented and intelligent friend back in Ventura. Frisbee Freeland Chew, III. He was then a self-employed foreign car mechanic, music lover, and political activist. We met at meetings of the Ventura Safe Energy Council. That group worked against nuclear power plants. Buddy, as we all called him, came from the perspective of a Libertarian, not an environmentalist. To him it made no sense economically to use nuclear power. It has taken about 40 years to convince the rest of the world of that. He got me thinking about politics in a different way and I eventually became a registered Libertarian for 15 years. I finally decided that was not working, switched to the Democrats and am now Decline to State but not pleased with much except art and music. Buddy was able to drop everything and drive up to Monterey the next day.

We set up the Park Stage, as it was called at the time. That was the first year of what would become the Garden Stage. The Night Club also opened for the first time that year. A photo of me with Jason and Buddy shows me coiling a mic cable, over/under. I taught Buddy how to do that and we were set to go. The Park Stage was very primitive. No carpets or drapes. A bare concrete stage and a few signs hung on the back wall. We plugged all the amps into outlets on the back wall. We had mics, stands and cables and I drew out custom stage plots for each band on my yellow legal pad. We filled up all twelve channels. That system worked for several years until we slowly outgrew it.

The Park Stage and Night Club schedules were printed in the program for the first time. The Park Stage had Benny Barth Trio at 6:00 on Friday, Dave Clay at noon on Saturday, Broadway Blues Band at 5:30 on Saturday night, Dave Clay again at 11:30 on Sunday followed by Vernon Alley Trio at 5:00 on Sunday. Benny Barth is the only set I photographed. I must have been too busy to shoot the others.

CLIPPING AND PHOTO BY J. NICHOLS: (bottom) BACK STAGE WALL

BACKSTAGE

PHOTO BY J. NICHOLS

PHOTO BY SUZKA: JIM AND LESLIE MERICAL

9
JIM AND LESLIE MERICAL 1986

John Nichols brought my husband Jim & I to Monterey Jazz Festival in 1986 to "help out" on the Garden Stage. Jim's experience as a musician, doing sound for friends and calm nature encouraged John to include us. It was a whole new world, this group of people who'd been coming together once a year – some for almost 30 years, to make the festival come to life. We were indoctrinated into the crew, a wild bunch, who spent the 1st day or so catching up on what had gone on in everyone's lives over the year, while ingesting the latest cocktail or spirit of the week, preparing the stages and immersing ourselves in the music that brought us all together. Joining this diverse "once-a-year" family, connected by the thread of Jimmy Lyons' and Paul Vieregge's Monterey Jazz Festival production, felt like "coming home." We were immediately hooked.

A few years after joining the stage crew, Mike Wilmot asked me if I'd like to be stage manager for the Jazz Theater. It wasn't a terribly taxing job. After the initial scramble to prepare the room & set hundreds of folding chairs, most of the time I was sitting in the dark. It was a great way to experience the festival, hosting the speakers, musicians and filmmakers whose movies we screened at the theater, playing music between sets, helping attendees feel welcome, making sure we didn't miss a beat coming from the live main stage feed, keeping amorous lovers from taking advantage of the cloak of darkness at the back of the theater and assisting any famous VIPs who came by to talk or watch. Mike Wilmot trusted me to pull it off without a hitch . . . most of the time!

Around 2007 (I think), I had a panel speaking following a movie, and I was told my special guest was going to be Clint Eastwood! It was the year I'd received a batch of folding chairs with more than a couple "weak ones". It was a packed house for the event, with many key board members and top brass showing up. More than once I was reminded to "take good care" of Mr. Eastwood!

It was pitch dark when Clint came up to me, mentioning he'd prefer to sit with us behind the soundboard, rather than in the chair I'd placed for him in the audience. The room was completely packed to the back wall. I ran to fetch a chair where I'd stashed a few extras, taking time to test a few by sitting in them with all my might.

Back at the soundboard, I gestured for him to have a seat.

It's a long way down when you're an icon over 6 feet tall. Watching as he sat down, I'm not sure if, in the darkness he missed the back of the chair, or if the chair was flawed, but I realized the chair wasn't holding him and I wasn't able to grab him fast enough as the chair, and Clint, collapsed on the ground with a loud crash!

I was horrified, and extremely concerned for him. Although he was still moving quite spryly, he had some miles on him and the fall briefly took his breath away. After ascertaining he wasn't bleeding or terribly injured, I reached down and pulled him to his feet. He was understandably shaken, but good-natured, and assured me he was all right. I felt everyone's eyes on us and knew it was a major faux pas. I was sure I'd instantly be relieved of my position, having failed my most important task that year.

Instead, Clint took to leaping aside whenever he saw me, declining my good natured offers "to take a seat", and for years the crew, board members & office staff took every opportunity to ask me if I'd thrown Clint down again! More than a few times, Mike Wilmot would come by, scan the crowd, and ask if I'd offered Clint any broken chairs.

PHOTO BY SUZKA: ALBERT CRISTY

10

ALBERT CRISTY 1989

On the Crews

    I came out to Salt Lake City from Rochester, New York to attend Westminster College in 1973. Directionless with little ambition like Amelia, I had a dream to fly. Westminster had a flying school and, hey... they had a music program, a jazz band. I'd been playing trombone since third grade, I could play in the jazz band. So I signed up. About twenty minutes after I sat down with the band I realized several things. One, I didn't really know anything about playing music. Two, I was way outclassed by these cats. And three, this was a kind of jazz I had never heard before. So I did the logical thing. I dug in and faked it.

As it turned out the band under the direction of Ladd McIntosh was recognized as one of the best college bands in the country. Many stars in the genre came in from time to time to jam with the best players in the band and give clinics. George Shearing, Clark Terri, Jean Luc Ponty, Tom Scott, and Frank Zappa all showed up while I was in attendance. But really the most important thing that happened as far as my life was concerned was meeting two life long friends; David Asman and Greg Floor.

On the jazz tour in January 1974 Greg became a coordinator as well as a performer. He was into drama and production and so he organized the 'conga line' to load and unload the tour bus. At the end of our shows we did an arrangement of 'Hey Jude' and as we filed out into the audience improvising all the way, Greg would walk out from the wings and do a bit of wild dancing. It always got the audience on their feet.

Over my four years at the college I gradually got to know Greg better. I saw him perform in dramatic productions with the college theater. I worked a bit in set building and helped with the last 'Mayfest' show, putting up Greg's portable stage at the end of the football field and switching out the acts. We also took that stage up to Park City to put on what turned out to be the first two primitive productions of the Park City Jazz festival.

Upon my graduation from Westminster Greg came by and told me that the little shotgun apartment downstairs from him was available for $75.00 a month! I leaped and became Greg's and his future wife, Jan's neighbor in 1977.

About a year later Greg came to me with the following proposal: Buy a ticket for the next Monterey Jazz Festival. Caravan out there in our VW buses, see the show, and meet "everyone" and then we'll go north, climb some mountains and have a vacation. Well my job had folded and I had saved a lot of money. I had the time to do this so I bought a ticket to see the 21st annual Monterey Jazz Festival.

We did everything just as planned. I managed to get out to the fairgrounds, only getting lost once. I parked my bus way out in the back end. I met everyone, Jimmy, Laurel, Paul, Mike and the crew, and I got to see Dizzy and Dexter Gordon play. Afterwards, we went up and climbed around on Mt. Shasta and Mt. Hood. We had a nice picnic afternoon on the shoulder of Mt. Saint Helens, trucked up to Tacoma and made a failed attempt to summit Mt Reiner. We traveled out to eastern Washington and picked apples for a week. It was one of the best vacations I ever had.

After that...well life happened. Jobs changed, money came and went. I was occupied. But every year Greg would come back from the coast and tell me, "Paul, Penny, and everyone wants to know when Albert is coming back." Hold on, how did I make such an impression? It seemed like just a few moments to me. Is the festival that hard up?

Finally, in 1989 I had the place, time, and money so I packed up and drove out. At that time we all camped in the back of the grounds where the concession people now park their RV's and trailers. So I pitched the tent and went to work. We set the wall and painted. We hung the set pieces and ate squid on the wharf. During the show I 'dressed' the curtain and helped out as best as a near total rookie could. I monitored the tape machine under the stage that recorded the show for the archives. Not a real hard gig so I had spare time. I took lots of pictures. Herbie Mann, Etta James, Charlie Musselwhite, Freddie Hubbard, Dizzy, and Take Six made it into my slide reels. I'm not sure but I think at the crew party after the show Mike Wilmot told me if I came back next year there 'might be a paycheck.' So I did.

For the '90 show, as I remember, I helped others on the main stage. I learned how to set the drums up on the risers, mike them, and I witnessed a few things. Dizzy had a cream colored leather suit that year and he wore it to the crew (then crew) barbecue. Coming through the line he was standing on the serving side with that suit on. I mimed "nice suit!" to him and he did the 'half closed eyes deep bow of the head' to me. Wow, I was recognized. Later during the show, Oscar Peterson was performing what turned out to be his last pre-stroke visit to the festival. He was winging through this solo blending jazz and classical riffs. I noticed that everyone back stage had stopped talking and was listening intently to him. When he stopped and the rest of the band kicked back in everyone back stage yelled and applauded—wonderful.

Stan Getz played his last that year. He was dying and not too many people knew it. His last tune was rolling and out of nowhere

Dizzy ran out on stage with that suit on and starts singing. That brought the house down. Riots of laughter and a standing ovation went on as the curtain clooed. Then the curious happened. We were all tearing down stuff and moving equipment and risers. Dizzy and Stan were standing almost front center stage not six inches between their faces having a very serious discussion oblivious to all else. Finally Paul gently walked up and asked them if they would mind moving the conversation off stage. Dizzy glanced around as if realizing where he was, grabbed Stan's arm and hussled off. I think Stan died that November. Dizzy left us January of 1993 Did they both know? I can only guess.

Life happened again in a large way. I missed the '92 show and as I heard, it was somewhat bitter sweet. I had just became employed with the local transit company. I was going through my probation period and I couldn't justify asking for vacation time that I didn't merit.

PHOTO BY J. NICHOLS: ALBERT CRISTY

I was back in 1993 and went to the Garden Stage where I have remained ever since. The more intimate vibe of the Garden has made the 'rubbing elbows' aspect a more common thing.

Trading Firesign Theater lines with Joe Zawinul's drummer. "Oh you must mean the old same place. It's around back, here's the key."

"I had a key but I had to split it with the sound effects man."

Telling Diana Krall where the bathroom was, pretty much watching Kyle Eastwood grow up, fixing Sarah McKenzie's dress so she didn't walk back out on stage with her butt hanging out, holding Mavis Staples hands and guiding her off stage while congratulating her on the show (hey, is she checking me out?) running out several times to fix Maceo Parker's drummers kit that he was doing his best to destroy and then having him thank me for all my hard work. Sitting next to Quincey Jones and listing to him talk to John Nichols was a recent highlight. I found out rather early on that the folks who come to do their thing on our stages are really just people. They are indeed very talented people, but they appreciate being treated as just folks and are thankful for the things we do to make their stay on stage a good one.

Out and about back home in Salt Lake people sometimes comment on the Monterey clothing. I have collected a lot of shirts, hats, and jackets over the years. They point and say, "That's neat, what's that chair mean?" or, "What's the Monterey Jazz festival?" I usually say, "That's just a job I do in September."

But every once in a while it goes like the time I was waiting in line at Home Depot, "You've been to the Monterey Jazz Festival?"

"Yeah, I've worked on the stage crew for over twenty years."

"Can I touch you? I've always wanted to go to that show."

It's then that I get the same feeling that I get when I walk up on the main stage on Sunday morning to clean and set the backdrop and begin the week of preparation for the weekend, a little pride, a feeling of honor, and a great sense of gratitude. I don't know how much longer I can do the show. There have been many years when I think this is my last one. Then spring comes along in the Wasatch, I catch a whiff of salt air off the lake and I start to think about what I need to bring with me this year. How is Penny doing? How many more days before I can hit the coast!

JOHN NICHOLS AND ALBERT CRISTY

KIM CANDLER

11

KIM CANDLER 1992

    I started attending the Monterey Jazz Festival in 1988w/boyfriend Jeremy Slate. He was working the Garden stage then. Of course I went with him every year until 1994 when I got a job at the jazz festival as stage crew on a new venue called Dizzy's Den. I was eight months pregnant with my daughter True. All of the stage crew members and our stage manager all from Big Sur. We were the furthest away from everything, always ended up wrapping-up, being done by 2am. Mike Wilmot coming down helping us wrap cords. I will never ever wrap a cord without thinking about Mike Wilmot. Paul Vieregge would always come down as well and check on us. I think it was for the pizza but he always did come and check on us. I have lots of precious moments of times I got to spend sitting with Paul and Penny. It was such a wonderful experience to be working at Dizzy's, that stage where you felt like you were totally part of the family, even the artist felt like part of your family. It's such a beautiful wonderful job to have. It is the best job I've ever done and I look forward to it every year.

My daughter True was there with us every year. Sometimes doing her homework with the artists and then going off to go to sleep. When the artist we're getting ready to go onstage they would come to me and say where is True? She promised to watch our show and me. Her father would have to explain that she had to go to bed. One time we sent her to the main stage to pick something up and bring it back to us and she walked in and there was Herbie Hancock. He turned around and saw her nametag on her pass and told her she had a beautiful name and asked her if she was enjoying the jazz festival and she said that she did not like jazz at all. Then she decided to ask the gentleman what his name was. He said I'm Herbie Hancock and she said 'oh my gosh I'm so sorry' He said don't worry I didn't like jazz when I was your age either.

There are so many more stories but I don't want to take up this book with all my stories all I can say is I'm so happy and proud to be part of this family I just attended the last Monterey Pop Festival 50 year anniversary and realized how much good work we all really do and the love everywhere. None of this awesomeness would have happened if it weren't for Paul Vieregge and Mike Wilmot. I love and miss them both so very much.

– Kim Candler

PHOTO BY SUZKA: KASIA

12
KASIA ZAJAC 1992

It was the first year of Dizzy's Den. A very significant year: Kim was pregnant with True, and I was just married and legal in America. I tried to do as good a job as I could not to be given too many evil eyes by Greg every time I did not understand what killing the house meant.

The very first day of Dizzy's was the Organ Summit. It was a dream that came true: Alan with his blue Hammond, carefully wrapped in a blanket; Pete Fallico in a gold suit as a Master of a Battle; the Battle itself. I don't remember a better double Hammond jam than that one. Dr Lonnie was having a blast playing more and more playfully, challenging musicians that sat down at the other Hammond: Larry Goldings seemed upset as if he was having a hard time keeping up with the doctor, and Bill Heid was looking very happy playing long solos that allowed him to send special smiles to all Asian women he could spot in the audience. It was a true live music.

The real test for new Dizzy's crew came on Sunday, though. The

BACKSTAGE

cleanup started inconspicuously: coiling cables and taking drums back stage. Well, some time later (could it be 2am? or later?) Mike Wilmot came looking for us with a leftover pizza from the party. We were just getting ready to start rolling the carpets, after having finished putting away all the chairs, and disassembling the stage. Along with the pizza, Mike also brought the checks. Barely standing from exhaustion in a perfectly empty room, I received my first official Jazz Fest salary: the best ever earned 100 dollars.

PHOTO BY SUZKA: ALEXANDER (above)
(below) DAVID PRICE

SUZKA

13

SUZKA 1993

It was on September 13, 1993 when I first stepped onto the main stage at the Monterey Fairgrounds becoming an official member of the stage crew for the Monterey Jazz Festival. I hadn't a clue what to expect. I was the outsider, the un-inherited crewmember moving into this sacred fraternity, but I was artistically prepared. I had painted 26 long canvases that would cover the back flats. Canvases I had previously painted on the street in front of my studio. Truck tire marks were visible on some of the canvases.

I was first introduced to Mike Wilmot - a tall sailor'd looking man with a sea worthy tan, a neatly trimmed beard and sandals. He was the stage manager. Mike interrupted a crowd standing in a huddle on the main stage. A crowd that last gathered for years in probably the same place at the previous festivals. They were 'The Crew'.

At the center front edge of the stage was a man with white hair and a fresh bruise over his right eye, siting on a metal chair reading the morning newspaper. He ran the show without running the show and appeared to be the overseer of all things holy and not so holy. The night before was the Jazz-eve's party at his cabin in Big Sur, probably the scene where the bruising took first appeared. His name was Paul Vieregge. I should have been nervous meeting such an icon but strangely enough, I wasn't. He made me feel like I was exactly where I was supposed to be.

"Hey kid. Let's see what ya got." I handed him the design of the backdrop 40 feet wide and 12 feet tall, scaled down that I had printed out the night before.

"Looks good. Welcome to the family." I wasn't sure if I needed to kiss his ring or what.

The crowd gathered around, all and looked at my design idea. Off to the side was one of the long rolls of painted canvas that sat on the stage floor like a pickle lying on a cheesecake. I don't think any of them were very impressed. One crewmember, a skinny looking character with a funny accent looked over my design and told me it was impossible. "This cannot be done. I don't want to be rude or hurt your feelings but this whole idea, hanging all these canvases is impossible." That was my first introduction to Cello. I only remember that somewhere I heard he was a big time engineer who designed the sewers in London. Hell, I went to London. I wasn't impressed with their sewers.

Mike Wilmot must have noticed I was a bit nervous. He told me, "You'll be fine. Your design looks great. We'll make it work." and gave me a warm confident smile. He was just so damn laid-back. Everybody was.

Mike and Paul were long time friends. They worked together at KGO-TV years ago. They were the heart of the festival. I believe they were a major part of why this crew kept coming back.

In addition to setting up the stages, there was mandatory, after-five, off-stage social activities that was part of this gig.

Monday night was football. Everyone gathered into one of the rooms at the Travel Lodge and watched whoever was playing on that particular night. It made no difference. This was a night for bonding, getting into the strategizing mindset, reinforcing positions and bird-dogging a target. A formation of alcohol was on the sideline to prevent any serious interference.

Tuesday night was slide show night on the main stage. That first year, Buddy Chew showed his slides of his hometown in Mammoth. I cannot remember a single image projected on the backstage wall that night but I do remember there were instructions unaware to the speaker. When Buddy used the word 'Mammoth' in his presentation, he were all to stand up, swing our left arm in the air as if it were an elephant's trunk. If he used the word 'snow', we were to throw marshmallows at him (marshmallows were provided). Slide shows had little to do with any photos or insight into someone's life back home. It was silly craziness and a traditional part of the Jazz festival as much as the performing music. In the later years Tuesday night was replaced with gathering in my studio in Sand City.

Wednesday was barbecue night in the earlier years. Now it's sushi. Saki replaced the beer and martini drinks.

Friday: Games on. Doors open.

SUZKA

That Saturday in 1993, the last sound checks on the main stage finished. I remember still having ample time to touch up the back stage set and clear out all the remaining paint cans before the curtains would open for the first act – the Dirty Dozen Brass Band. Everyone else was eating or getting a little bit of shuteye before the festival would open their gates. Tim came onto stage, complimented me on my work but also told me that I had forgotten to include the word 'festival' on the stage set. Festival was a big word to simply leave off, apparently. He told me that Mrs. Lyons was very upset. But he also told me that it was my choice to add it or not. He would back my decision either way. I gained a great deal of respect for Tim that day.

I was exhausted and began packing up. I started to carry out the remaining gallons of paint off the stage when in the corner of my eye I saw this little woman with a large cloth bag moving into the middle of the stage.

"See what she did…" The lady pulled opened her bag and angled its opening in such a way as if she were giving its contents full view of the stage, my stage. "Do you see what she did? Look!"

She moved the bag's opening from stage right to stage left giving its contents the full panoramic view of the entire stage wall. Slowly she moved her torso with bag and then abruptly paused at the end of the beautifully painted words 'Monterey Jazz'. That's when I felt this eerie cold air floating across the stage. I am an artist, 'Hungarian' artist with unspeakable lineage to gypsies. I had no control as to where my mind was traveling.

"Look closely. Do you see the word festival anywhere on this set? No you don't because it's not there. Now do you see what I'm talking about?" She was rather persistent in her disgust. "They changed the name, Jimmy! I'm not sure if that girl had something to do with this or not but this is wrong!"

I knew what she was doing and what she was carrying with her. Although I did not exactly see what was in her bag, the talk around the festival was that Mrs. Lyons was carrying her husband's ashes with her the entire weekend.

Sometime dead people can put a curse on you if they're upset about something. I wasn't going to take any chances. I added the word festival to the stage set and finished painting it just minutes before the curtain opened for the first act.

And about those canvases from my first stage design... I still have them, most of them. Years later I was asked to create a backdrop using those very canvases for a film about the history of the Monterey Jazz Festival. Clint Eastwood was the producer. It was sometime in 1996. I hauled about 10 of those long canvases down to Eastwood's Studio at Warner Brothers in Hollywood. It was an absolute huge warehouse completely empty with wood rafters, which were far higher than my ladder's reach. But I couldn't think about any limitation at the time. I had only four hours to create something - a setting for the musicians who were to be filmed. This was my 'forte'.

Throughout the installation a tall gentleman off to the side caught my attention. He was wearing gray jeans, a white T with a cotton black jacket and bright red sneakers. I never saw red shoes like that before. They were so bright it was like those sneakers walked around the room by themselves. I felt comport knowing he was there even though we never met. He appeared approachable in case I needed some human (non-celebrity) contact.

I finished in just enough time. About 8 or 9 long canvases with splattered color hung from the rafters 12 feet in the air and crossed on the floor creating a circular cocoon of color. Additional canvases laid flat on the floor. A piano for Dave Brubeck was brought in and placed a bit off the center on top of the floored canvases. Stools were set about in no particular order. It looked great.

Clint Eastwood came into the building first followed by Joshua Redman then came Dave Brubeck, Joe Williams and Clark Terry. They walked into my world that I had hoped would be a perfect place to talk about Jazz, the Monterey Jazz Festival and of course play a little music. They loved it as well. At the end they got on the floor and signed the canvases. God, I was so thrilled.

That was also the day when I was properly introduced to Kyle Eastwood for the first time. He was wearing bright red sneakers.

BACKSTAGE

KIM CANDLER (upper left); CHELSEA DAVEY (right),
UNCLE GILES DAVEY and BABY TY (below)

BACKSTAGE

] DIZZY'S DEN OPENED IN 1995 [

THE DIZZY DEN'S NOTABLE CREW; (below) THEIR LEADER, GREG DAVEY

PHOTO BY J. NICHOLS: MIKE WILMOT

14
JOHN NICHOLS 1977

PHOTO BY J. NICHOLS

The Monterey Jazz Festival as The Hero's Journey

In Joseph Campbell's 1949 book, "The Hero With A Thousand Faces", he popularized the concept of a *Hero's Journey* with stages.

Campbell described the basic narrative pattern as follows:

A hero ventures forth from the world of common day into a region of supernatural wonder: fabulous forces are there encountered and a decisive victory is won: the hero comes back from this mysterious adventure with the power to bestow boons on his fellow man.

The *Hero's Journey* is a popular form of story structure sometimes called a *Monomyth*. This character arc can be overlayed onto the more traditional three-act structure that many Hollywood movies follow. Star Wars and The Wizard of Oz are examples. I have taken some of the relevant elements of the *Monomyth* and matched them up with what I have observed in my own life and the life of the Monterey Jazz Festival. MJF is definitely a *Special World*.

I grew up in the *Ordinary World* of Ventura, California and went to high school with Mike Wilmot. We were active in little theater and became friends. He rented a tux and was in my wedding. After his marriage to Sue they lived in a furnished apartment on the beach in Ventura. My wife Leslie and I moved into that old apartment when he and Sue moved on to San Francisco. We visited them on our honeymoon and remained friends. Mike got a job in San Francisco television and that lead to working on the crew at the Monterey Jazz Festival.

Soon after he started working at the festival he began asking me if I wanted to come up and work with him on the crew. That was my *Call To Adventure*. Part of my preparation had been becoming a jazz fan at age 14 and collecting a lot of records and subscribing to Downbeat magazine. I wanted to be a beatnik. I attended the festival in 1963 and 1964.

PHOTO BY J. NICHOLS: MIKE WILMOT AND JOHN NICHOLS

Mike kept asking me to join the crew whenever we visited each other. Although it sounded interesting, I *Refused The Call* year after year. I had college to finish. After college I had a career in teaching 7th Grade science to get started. My 7th grade classes started the same week as work on the festival. Working at the festival just did not seem possible.

1977 was the year I broke loose from the *Ordinary World* for that first weekend at the Monterey Jazz Festival. That event was the *Crossing The Threshold*. I worked up the courage to leave my job for one day during the first week of school. Walking out of the classroom on Thursday afternoon was part of the crossing of a self-inflicted barrier to a life richer than classroom teaching. Arriving at the fairgrounds on Thursday evening in the middle of the party involved finding my way there with only vague directions from Mike. I could see and hear the party and walked through the chain link fence gate into the semi-darkness of the grass and trees and rows of BBQ pits.

I was anointed with a beer and nourished with some of Leon's ribs. I would later come to be aware of a man behind the curtain that we all paid attention to. There was also a lion but he was brave and a tin man with a big heart. There were lots of scarecrows who were all very intelligent. The party was swarming with fools and jesters and warriors with special belts and shoes and black shirts. Princes and princesses were mingling. I had entered a *Special World*.

I was introduced to Paul Vieregge. He had a full beard that year and was wearing the holey MJF T-shirt I would later adopt. I did not know it at the time but that was my *Meeting The Mentor* moment. I also did not know that that weekend was the beginning of my *Hero's Journey*.

I was not aware at the time that joining the crew at the festival was a journey. It was just fun and different than my *Ordinary World*. I had a background in theater from running the lights and curtain back stage in high school. From that experience I moved on to running the light board at a community theater. Acting did not appeal to me. Being a techie did.

In my *Ordinary World* of becoming a teacher I was surrounded by fellow teachers who had a goal of teaching for a few decades and then retiring. Some had the goal of morphing into the occupation of administrator. All the role models in my life at that time seemed to be other teachers. My wife, Leslie, was teaching and all our friends were teachers.

The *Special World* of the Monterey Jazz Festival revealed itself slowly over many years. The music is always the greatest I would hear and see all year. People back in Santa Paula would often ask me who was going to play or who did play. Hardly any name I would ever mention would ring a bell or convert a new fan to my new favorite band. I usually say something flip like, "Oh, the the bands just play background music for the stage crew's annual party". That's not to denigrate the quality of the music but just to point out that jazz and the other types of music played at the festival are not going to be found easily in our pop dominated TV culture. The music is an element of the *Elixir* that takes the crew and the audience deeper into the **Special World** of the Monterey Jazz Festival. We all come out changed and invigorated to renew our quest to create a better world for ourselves and the next generation.

An essential part of the journey that the crew lives through are the *Tests, Allies and Enemies* we encounter. My first five years were weekends only. I would have to wait to experience the magical transformations that occur during an entire week before the performances. During those first weekends I had great experiences and learned not to drop microphones but did not connect deeply with the rest of the crew. That all changed when I left teaching and could experience the entire week of the festival.

On that first full week I drove up the coast from Ventura and somehow found my way down Sycamore Canyon and over the bridge to Paul and Penny's Big Sur home. I drank a lot and slept on a couch. On Sunday we relaxed and walked to the beach. I got to know my allies and they got to know me. Physical labor started on Monday but I came to know that the *Great Work* had already begun.

Besides building the walls, painting the set, moving the piano and sweeping up the pigeon shit we all needed to eat and drink. We were on the road so that meant breakfast, lunch and dinner out with the crew. That's a good way to get to know people better. The *Tests* I encountered were fun for me. I got to climb tall ladders and paint designs on walls that looked great from the audience and talk, talk and talk. This was a world different than classroom teaching and my jazz crew allies taught me by example. I was slowly building my confidence and preparing myself for the greater challenges that would come in my future at the festival.

By 1983 I figured I was in the groove with working on the crew. Build the walls, paint the set, run the show. That was the year the festival started selling out the main arena. Paul took me aside at a party on Monday night and told me that the festival was adding a few bands to the Park Stage and would be selling Grounds Passes for $10 each to people who could not get into the main arena. He would like me to be the stage manager of that stage. I was pleased and shocked. How could someone of my limited experience in jazz festivals pull off that job? That's when I conquered one of my *Enemies*, self-doubt. I said, "Sure". Since I would need a crew I got on the phone and called Frisby Freeland Chew, III, a friend from Ventura. He was single, a self-employed foreign car mechanic and smart enough to do anything. He drove up the next day. I walked over to the drug store and bought a clip board binder, some paper and pens and I was set.

"Buddy" Chew and I ran the Park Stage and Jason Slate, Jeremy's brother, ran the sound board. We hung a sign on the back wall and were in business.

The *Ordeal* of developing the Park Stage venue into what became the Garden Stage was mercifully gradual. For the first few years we just plugged the amps into the wall sockets on the back wall. We learned to coil mic cables over and under. There were no drapes or carpet so it sometimes sounded like we were playing inside a metal box. We slowly learned how to run this particular stage.

Years went by. The technical challenges grew. We added better sound, stage power and a light board. We added carpet for better sound and drapes. Albert Cristy joined the crew. Later we added Jim Merical who had been one of my 7th grade students. Jim brought along his wife Leslie and then Marty Van Loan. Others came and went.

After 20 years of the Garden Stage I decided to celebrate by creating a special post card. The message was: "Garden Stage - 20th Anniversary - The Pedagogy of Repetition". I stole that slogan from a cooking show I had seen on TV. Cooks learn how to chop carrots and do other tasks by repetition. Chop 1,000 onions and you magically become better at chopping onions. It's not reading about it or thinking about it or watching it. It's in the repeating of good practices where the transformation occurs.

Ordeals were overcome by long years of repetition. There were also changes occurring by the act of the *Approach To The Inmost Cave*. I can't speak for the rest of the crew but in my personal case I could not have overcome the *Ordeals* that were presented to me without exploring my own personal cave. In order to be more effective on the crew of the Monterey Jazz Festival I needed to become more effective in my own life in Santa Paula. I did that with the help of another mentor, Marjorie Leaming. She was my minister at the Universalist Unitarian Church of Santa Paula. I would visit her and talk for an hour once a week and interpret my dreams and journal. I needed a lot of help to make that transition from being a teacher to being self-employed and developing my new career as an artist / gallery owner / curator / book dealer / writer / picture framer / antique dealer / stage manager. I wasn't going to be able to run a better stage at the Monterey Jazz Festival unless I could run a better self on the conscious and unconscious levels back home in the *Known Reality*. The *Ordeals* of the Known and the Unknown portions of my reality manifested themselves both at the festival and at home. It became important to understand the unconscious.

What about the *Rewards?* What about the *Seizing of the Sword?* How am I supposed to measure my progress on all fronts unless I can hold up my *Rewards* to show the world what I have accomplished? I have a collection of over 40 T-shirts. I have a collection of over 40 crew badges from the Monterey Jazz Festival. I rest my case.

I load up my car at the end of the festival each year and take *The Road Back*. I bring the Monterey Jazz Festival back with me to my *Ordinary World*. The road goes both ways and from what I can tell I have taken as much away from the festival as I have given. The Monterey Jazz Festival has given much to my *Ordinary World*.

There is proof of this in the *Resurrection*. Every year on the third weekend in September the Monterey Jazz Festival occurs. It takes shape based on the primary genetic code of jazz but is ever evolving to meet the needs of the current human condition. In addition to the sound waves being produced for the awed crowd there are multiple waves of vibrations on all the many levels of existence that we experience directly and indirectly. This interdependent web of all existence of which we are all a part vibrates with the sounds of jazz and sends the positive vibrations out to not only the rest of our world but on to the *Next Generation*. I have experienced that Resurrection Hymn over and over again in my life not only in the *Special World* of the Monterey Jazz Festival but all throughout the years as I live out my life in the *Ordinary World*.

Every year I return home with the *Elixir* from the Monterey Jazz Festival as a changed person. I return to the place where I began my journey but things will never be the same.

BACKSTAGE

BACKSTAGE

ADDITIONAL PHOTOS…

BACKSTAGE

MARY VIEREGGE

PHOTOS BY J. NICHOLS: (above) 'Jazz Camp' JIM MERICAL, BUDDY CHEW, JOHN NICHOLS, LESLIE MERICAL, GREG FLOOR w. 76VW Camper, (below) Jazz Crew Barbeque

PHOTO BY J. NICHOLS: PAUL VIEREGGE

BACKSTAGE

PHOTO BY J. NICHOLS: PAUL VIEREGGE, WILMOT, MANSHIP

PHOTO BY J. NICHOLS: JEROEN AND PAUL

PHOTO BY J. NICHOLS: MILT FRANKEL
Prince of Darkness

BACKSTAGE

PHOTO BY J. NICHOLS: GREG FLOOR

BACKSTAGE

PHOTOS BY J. NICHOLS

PHOTO BY J. NICHOLS

BACKSTAGE

PHOTO BY J. NICHOLS: (above) JOEL WILMOT, GREG FLOOR
(below) GREG DAVEY, ALBERT, SUZKA

PHOTO BY J. NICHOLS: GILES DAVEY

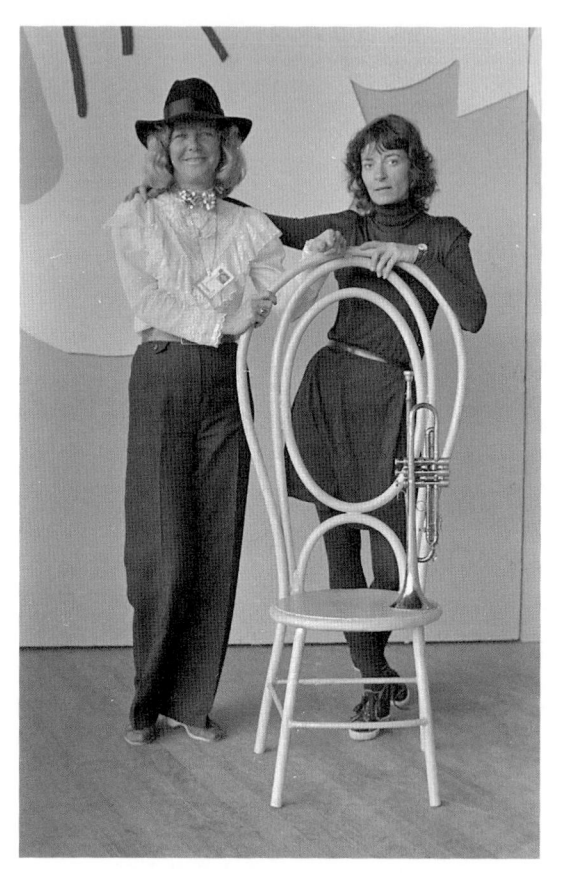

PHOTO BY J. NICHOLS: BRENDA WEISS AND MORGAN

BACKSTAGE

PHOTO BY J. NICHOLS: CHELSEA

GREG FLOOR AND BO DIDDLY

PHOTO BY J. NICHOLS: LESLIE AND JIM MERICAL, PENNY VIEREGGE

PHOTO BY J. NICHOLS: THE GARDEN STAGE CREW

CREW'S 'BIG NIGHT' DINNER AT SUZKA'S WAREHOUSE

PHOTO BY J. NICHOLS: GREG FLOOR, JOEL WILMOT

PHOTO BY J. NICHOLS: CHELSEA

BACKSTAGE

SUZKA, JOEL   (above) SUZKA, FLOOR   ILENE, RENATA

GREG DAVEY
(below)

BACKSTAGE

2018 - (left to right from top) MIKE MANSHIP, JOEL WILMOT, CELLO, LESLIE MERICAL, J.O., KIM CANDLER, JIM MERICAL, SUZKA

BACKSTAGE

TIM JACKSON

BACKSTAGE

BACKSTAGE

BACKSTAGE

02-06-18

Printed in Great Britain
by Amazon